UNWELCOME VISITOR

The quiet of the sunlit night was interrupted by a splashing sound. The Hardys looked up to see a large brown bear waddling toward them.

"Is it a grizzly?" Joe whispered.

"Looks like it," Frank answered, glancing at the fire. "It probably smelled the fish. Where'd you put the guts?"

"I threw them in the—" Joe stopped suddenly, staring. The fish guts had landed on a nearby rock.

The bear went right to the fish guts. In one gulp, he licked them up. Then, twitching his nose, he headed for what was left of the fish beside the fire.

"He's coming nearer," Joe whispered, eyes wide.

The bear abruptly rose up on its hind legs, throwing a long shadow that fell like night over the boys.

Then the unnatural silence was shattered with one giant roar as the grizzly began its charge!

Books in THE HARDY BOYS CASEFILES® Series

Available from ARCHWAY Paperbacks

TROUBLE IN THE PIPELINE

FRANKLIN W. DIXON

AN ARCHWAY PAPERBACK
Published by POCKET BOOKS
New York   London   Toronto   Sydney   Tokyo

AN ARCHWAY PAPERBACK *Original*

An Archway Paperback published by
POCKET BOOKS, a division of Simon & Schuster Inc.
1230 Avenue of the Americas, New York, NY 10020

ISBN: 0-671-64689-3

First Archway Paperback printing April 1989

10 9 8 7 6 5 4 3 2 1

TROUBLE IN THE PIPELINE

Chapter

1

"WILL YOU STEP on it, Frank? We're late." Joe Hardy strained forward against his seat belt and twisted the dial on the radio in their van. His blond hair was still wet and was combed straight back. In clean chinos and a Hawaiian shirt, he was dressed for a party. He found a station he liked and sat back, arms folded, to glare impatiently at his older brother.

"Calm down," Frank said, turning into a narrow road in a quiet section of Bayport. "Don't you know it's fashionable to be late?"

"Being late is one thing—missing half the party is another," Joe grumbled.

Frank chuckled. Put girls and food in front of Joe Hardy, and watch out! Keeping his dark eyes on the road, Frank said, "It'll be good to see

1

Doug. It's been almost three years, between his army stint and then that job in Alaska.''

Joe stirred restlessly, staring out the side window. "We'll be lucky if there's any food left. I know Lisa invited a lot of people."

"The party is for Doug Hopkins, Joe—not your stomach," said Frank. "I hope we'll be able to get to talk to the guest of honor in the mob scene."

"We'll find out in a minute." Frank was driving at an easy pace. The road was narrow and curvy as it led through a large suburban development— small houses, each with a "Children at Play" warning on the lawn. The late-summer evening was breezeless and cool. Frank didn't feel like hurrying. His girl, Callie Shaw, couldn't make the party, and he wasn't eager to go without her.

A car was coming from the opposite direction, and Frank snugged up next to the curb under a streetlight to let it pass. Instead, the green two-door slammed to a stop beside him, and the driver leaned out his window. He wore a gray work shirt and a heavy growth of stubble on his face.

"Hey, kid," the man asked. "Where's Christensen Drive?"

"You just passed it," Frank answered. "Three blocks back, make a right, then look for a dead end. We're heading there our—"

Before he could finish, the guy slammed the car into first. Tires screeching, the car whipped through a tight U-turn, then barreled past the

Hardys' van. Frank stared as the car swerved, narrowly missing a little kid's bike that had been left against the curb. The green car roared up onto somebody's lawn, cutting a set of dirt tire tracks through the grass, and disappeared.

"Those morons!" Joe pounded the dashboard as he watched the taillights flash up the block, then make a shrieking right turn.

"Did you get their license plate?" Frank asked, his arms crossed on the steering wheel.

"License plate? I barely saw them!" Joe said.

Starting the van's engine, Frank said, "Lisa lives on Christensen Drive. We may bump into those guys again."

"If I catch those bozos, I'll burn rubber, too— right on their heads." He glanced over at Frank. "Well? Aren't we going?"

"That depends," his older brother replied. "Are we heading for the party, or are you out looking for trouble?"

"Will you knock it off and get us to Lisa's? We were supposed to be there an hour ago."

They had to park the van half a block from Lisa Shannon's house because a dozen cars already lined both curbs. They could hear the beat of music pounding down the street as they strolled under the dark canopy of trees. No one noticed them walk in. People were dancing or standing around in groups, talking and laughing. Joe headed straight for the dining room table. Frank watched as his brother slapped together a huge

3

salami and cheese sandwich, and he shook his head.

With Joe distracted, Frank decided he'd better represent the Hardy family and say hello. He went to look for Lisa or Doug.

Lisa had gone all out; her house was jammed. People were there to celebrate Doug's homecoming *and* the end of summer. Finally, out on the patio, Frank found Doug sitting quietly in the dark on a wicker couch.

"So, here's the man of the hour!" Frank said, grinning as he sat down next to him.

Doug looked up and smiled sheepishly, shaking back his light brown hair. He was sitting on the edge of the seat, leaning forward with his elbows on his knees. Always a good athlete in high school, Doug looked even more fit and sturdy than Frank remembered him.

"How does it feel to be back in civilization?" Frank asked.

"Okay." Doug shrugged.

"Well, we're glad to have you back. I guess the size of this bash shows how happy Lisa is."

"Yeah, it's great." Doug sat back and rubbed his hands together.

Frank stared. Was Doug trying to brush him off? Or were the one-word answers a sign of something going on between Doug and Lisa?

"Everything's okay between you guys?"

"Sure," said Doug, not changing his expression.

4

"Lisa was so proud of you. She talked about your job in Alaska all summer. I guess it's a good way to build up a nest egg."

If Frank thought he had found an opening, he was in for disappointment. Doug didn't respond.

"So, how was it?" Frank found himself getting a little embarrassed. "You must be tired of answering that question."

"It was okay," Doug said flatly.

"What'd you do?"

"I worked for a company that maintains the Alaska oil pipeline. I cleared land, cut brush—that kind of thing." Doug turned away, reaching for a soda on the end table.

"What's the summer like up there?"

"Pretty warm during the day, but at night it got cold. We were in Prudhoe, you know, up on the north coast—right on the Arctic Ocean. It stayed light all night long. You could read outdoors at any time just by the light from the sun."

Frank laughed. "That must be weird. I'd have trouble sleeping, I think."

Doug nodded. "Yeah, at first you do. But you get used to it."

"Didn't you go up there with one of your army buddies?" Frank asked.

If Doug had been warming up, that question cooled him down. His face became a mask; only his eyes moved, darting back and forth.

"I went with my pal Scott. We worked together," he finally answered in a measured beat.

Lisa Shannon came out onto the patio just then. She was a tall, dark-haired girl with a round face and a brilliant, warm smile. But Frank noticed that she seemed almost timid as she approached Doug. "Want to dance?" she asked after smiling at Frank.

Doug barely looked up. "No, thanks," he grunted. Lisa raised an eyebrow, smiled slightly, and backed away.

"Okay. If you change your mind, I'll be in the kitchen, making some dip."

Frank waited until Lisa had gone. "Come on, Doug, something's bothering you. You're acting as if this were your funeral, not a homecoming."

Doug shot him a look of pure terror, then he quickly recovered. "Just tired, I guess." He managed a nervous little laugh, but he wasn't acting like the Doug that Frank knew.

Doug was older than Frank and Joe, but he'd always been very friendly and outgoing. And even though he'd been a few years ahead of them in school, he'd spent a lot of time hanging out at their house and talking to their father. Fenton Hardy had a reputation as one of the best detectives in the country, and Doug was very interested in police work.

After high school Doug had enlisted in the army, and when his tour of duty was over, he had gone up to Alaska to have one last adventure before settling down. The adventure seemed to have turned Doug into a nervous wreck.

Frank wasn't about to try interrogating a friend. He stood up and stretched once. "I think I'll try some of that dip. Catch you later." He turned and followed the thumping of the music back into the living room. Joe had finished eating and was now starting to occupy himself with girls. He was dancing with a redheaded one in a white dress. Frank smiled at the girl and tapped Joe on the shoulder.

"Can I talk to you?"

"Not *now*." Joe made it very clear that he wanted to be left alone.

Frank raised his shoulders in a shrug and stepped off, thinking that maybe that business with the maniac driver had put Joe on edge.

Frank headed for the dining room and loaded a paper plate with chips and dip. Then he stepped back out to the patio. Doug was gone, his glass of soda half-empty on the table beside the wicker couch. Frank left his plate and walked around the side of the house to look for Doug.

The green car that had stopped them for directions was parked on the street, blocking the driveway. The driver and passenger were out of the car, standing on either side of Doug. Both were big, brawny types and loomed over him.

Whatever Doug said must have annoyed them. The driver suddenly grabbed Doug's arms, pinning them back. The other guy sank his fist into Doug's gut in a vicious body punch.

Chapter

2

FRANK WAS SMART. He stepped back into the dancing crowd, grabbed Joe, and hauled him outside.

"What are you—" Joe began. Then, by the porch lights, he saw the two guys working Doug over. Joe and Frank raced up to them. The driver with the heavy stubble was still holding Doug. Joe grabbed the guy's shoulder and whirled him around. With the goon's grip broken, Doug sagged to the ground, barely conscious. Frank knelt to make sure he was all right as the second guy began to retreat.

"Hey, Whiskers, what's going on here?" Joe demanded of the guy with the stubble.

"None of your business," Whiskers snarled, backing up.

"I think it is," Joe shot back. "You drive like

8

a maniac, now you beat up on a friend of ours. I think the cops—''

The two strong-armed men began retreating faster. Joe dashed after them, only to be stopped by the driver's heavy boot applied none too gently to his midsection. Frank leapt to his feet and was knocked down instantly by a chop to his throat that left him gasping for air.

The thugs, at their car by now, jumped in, gunned the engine, and tore off, leaving a strip of rubber on the street.

''You okay?'' Joe asked, helping Frank up.

''Yeah,'' Frank rasped. ''Another inch and he'd have crushed my throat. How's Doug?''

Doug struggled to his feet, moving like a broken old man. His lower lip was split. Frank pulled the van down to the driveway, and Joe helped Doug onto the passenger seat. They didn't want any of the partygoers seeing him like that.

''Who were those guys?'' Joe asked.

Doug shook his head. ''Don' wanna tawk,'' he managed, dribbling blood.

''Come on, Doug. You've got to tell us. We can help you if you're in trouble.'' Frank handed Doug a handkerchief. ''What did they want?''

Dabbing at his lip and chin, Doug gave them a you-won't-believe-this look. ''They warned me to forget about what happened in Alaska.''

Frank and Joe exchanged glances. What could be so important that two thugs would come all the way to Bayport from Alaska? "Okay. What happened?" Frank asked.

"Scott and I found out that some managers in the company we were working for were taking bribes. And like stupid idiots, we told a higher-up, thinking he'd want to know. We thought we'd get promotions."

Joe raised his eyebrows. "Didn't turn out that way?"

"The guy said he'd investigate—next thing we know, a bunch of thugs grabbed us." Doug looked up at the Hardys, exhausted and terrified. "They threw me on a plane and said if I talked to anyone, anyone at all, they'd kill me." He hung his head. "I don't even know what happened to Scott."

"You mean he didn't go home?"

"I called his folks, pretending to be another army buddy. They told me he was still in Alaska. I had overheard some of the guys who grabbed us talking. They were interested in Scott because he knew a lot about explosives. He was a demolitions expert in the army."

"What's the name of this company you worked for?"

"Trans-Yukon Mining. But they also do construction and maintenance work on the pipeline. Everyone up there does some."

"Did those two come from Alaska?"

"No. They said mutual friends in Alaska sent

them to check up on me. When I told them to leave me alone, they—''

Frank interrupted. ''What about those bribes? Who was spreading the money around? And *what* were they bribing people to do?''

Doug shook his head. ''I don't know. We just happened to overhear these managers talking about their new-found wealth, and they mentioned it was bribe money. They found out we had overheard, decided we knew more than we did, and that was it.''

He looked up at them, miserable. ''I thought I wanted to be a cop, but I don't think I could handle it. I can't handle this. Could you—can you go up to Alaska and find Scott—at least find out what happened to him?'' he added in a mere whisper. ''I'm really scared. You saw. These guys mean business.''

''We'll go,'' Frank said. ''We'll find Scott and get to the bottom of this bribery thing, too. Now, let's get you to a hospital. Then you'd better stay at our house, where you'll be safe until we get back.''

They took Doug to the emergency room and back to their house. Early the next morning the boys were in the air, heading for Alaska.

''Scott could be anywhere,'' Frank was saying as the plane droned its way toward Seattle, Washington. ''He could be a prisoner, or in hiding. He might even be working for those guys up there by now.''

"He could be dead." Joe cracked his knuckles and looked out at the peaceful blue and white of the cloud-lined sky.

They changed planes in Seattle, and in Fairbanks, Alaska, changed again. When they finally reached Prudhoe, they'd been in the air for almost twelve hours. They found the nearest motel and crashed. Although it was light outside, the town was in bed. And there was nothing they could do but sleep until morning.

The next morning they visited Trans-Yukon Mining. The company's offices were in a drab cinder-block building not far from Prudhoe's busy harbor on the Arctic Ocean. After getting past the receptionist, they found themselves in the outer office of the president of the company.

"We'd like to see Mr. Hammond." Joe leaned across the secretary's desk, turning on the charm. Frank never ceased to be amazed. Put a pretty girl in front of the guy and he became a different person. Joe's eyes sparkled with warmth and curiosity as he spoke. "My name is Joe Hardy. What's yours?"

"Cindy," the girl stammered. "Cindy Velikov." Drawn out of herself by the sheer force of Joe's smile, she shook hands. Joe held it for longer than necessary.

"Pleased to meet you, Cindy." He smiled cheerfully. "Think my brother and I could have a word with your boss?"

A blush spread across Cindy's pretty face to

the roots of her blond hair. "He—he doesn't like being disturbed. Do you have an appointment?"

"No. But we came all the way from New York to speak to him. We just want a few minutes of his time."

Cindy's ears perked up. "New York? I've never— Is it really like the pictures?"

"Oh, bigger!" Joe's hands made sweeping gestures. "Better!"

Cindy's blue eyes sparkled. "My dream is to live in New York, in one of those tall buildings with a doorman."

She hit some buttons on the intercom in front of her. "I'll check if Mr. Hammond can see you. Have a seat."

While they were waiting, Frank leaned over to Joe and whispered in his ear, "Let me handle this, okay? He may be clean, so I'm not going to hit him with everything we know."

Joe nodded.

Moments later they found themselves in Mr. Hammond's office. Dark wood paneling that matched the massive desk hid the cinder block here. A man rose, gesturing toward a pair of chairs. "I'm Spike Hammond," he said. "Sit down."

Hammond had the body of a man who'd done hard physical work all his life. In fact, he looked out of place in this office, as if he'd been stuffed into a suit and lowered in by a crane. His square jaw was balanced by an abundance of tousled red hair that fell low on his sunburned forehead. A scattering of freckles marched across the bridge of his nose.

"What brings you to Prudhoe?" Hammond asked.

Frank spoke up. "We're looking for a friend, Scott Sanders. He's supposed to be working for Trans-Yukon."

Hammond cocked his head to one side, then shook it as he leaned against his desk. "No. I don't recall that he does," he said.

"Here's a picture." Frank pulled out a snapshot of Scott in his army uniform.

Hammond took the photo between his thumb and forefinger. "Don't recognize the face; don't remember the name." He handed the picture back.

"Would you object if we had a look at your records?" Joe sat quietly with his hands folded in his lap. But Frank could hear the determination in his voice.

"That would be a bit unusual," Hammond said. "We don't normally allow anyone access to that information."

Frank jumped in. "We understand. But I don't see how you can rely on your memory to recall every name and face that passes through here."

Hammond chuckled, moving around to the other side of the desk. "I'm not one to forget a face."

"But we'd like to be sure," Joe interjected.

"We believe that Scott Sanders did work here and that he's now in some kind of trouble. I hope you'll help us out."

"I'd like to help." Hammond's forehead wrinkled in sympathy. "But it's company policy. I can't go around opening personnel records."

Frank took a deep breath. "Mr. Hammond, I'll be honest with you. We got some postcards from Scott, telling us that he was working here, and that he knew some of your managers were taking kickbacks. That's all we know. After a while the postcards stopped, and he didn't come home when he was supposed to. His folks are beginning to get nervous."

Hammond sat down. "You say this guy thought my managers were taking kickbacks? From whom?"

"He didn't say," Frank answered truthfully. "I doubt if he knew."

"Well, that's news to me." Hammond bit off his words. Frank couldn't decide if it was from anger, surprise, or the tension of a guilty conscience. "Thanks for the tip," Hammond said. "I'll look into it immediately." He got up and started to show them out. As they were passing Cindy Velikov she looked up and smiled.

"Sir, I overheard you say that Scott Sanders never worked here. But I remembered him, and I took the liberty of looking him up." She pointed to her computer screen. Joe moved quickly, not waiting for Hammond's reaction.

"He's on record," Joe said firmly. "Scott Sanders started work in June and 'quit' in mid-August." He quickly scanned the rest of Scott's personnel information, but there were no clues.

For a second the Hardys thought Hammond was going to explode with anger at Cindy. But he controlled himself and said simply, "I still don't think I ever heard that name—sorry."

Frank nodded, and Joe winked at Cindy. They left the office knowing only that Doug had told the truth. They weren't any closer to Scott.

There wasn't much to do in the Caribou Motel, where Frank and Joe were staying. They were lying on top of their beds fully clothed, including down parkas. Someone had forgotten to turn on the heat.

"Do we go to the police?" Joe asked, staring at a map of the area.

"I don't think so," Frank said. "That might scare whoever's involved—Scott may get hurt if he's still alive. Let's check around town for any kind of a clue to his whereabouts."

A faint knock on the door brought the Hardys sitting bolt upright. Frank ducked behind the door while Joe called out, "Who is it?"

"It's Cindy—Mr. Hammond's secretary," came a small voice from outside.

Joe opened the door to reveal a frightened Cindy. He made sure she was alone. "Are you all right?" he asked, staring at her.

"I have to tell you," she said. "Mr. Hammond was furious with me when I let you see my computer screen. Then I heard him on the phone. I don't know what's going on, but I think you'd better leave."

Frank came out from behind the door. "Why? What did he say?"

She was startled by Frank's sudden appearance. "I didn't hear everything, but he said something about 'getting rid' of you." Cindy stepped back, ready to bolt. "I can't stay—just be careful." She glanced around, terrified. "And don't tell anyone I talked to you. I just barely have my job still."

Joe sighed as he closed the door. "Do you think she'll be all right?"

"I'd worry more about us," Frank said. "Come on." In a few minutes they had piled up most of the furniture in front of the flimsy door.

They took turns standing guard, but the trip and jet lag caught up with Joe on his turn. He had just dozed off when he heard a crash. Four men smashed through the thin plasterboard of the room's back wall to fling both Hardys to the floor.

Joe was grabbed and shoved into a huge canvas bag—a mail sack, he guessed as he fought to get free. He might as well have been paralyzed. There was no way out of the heavy canvas.

Then came a blow to the back of his head—and the darkness in the bag gave way to deeper blackness.

Chapter

3

JOE CAME TO FIRST.

He was folded in half, lying on his side, and only when he tried to straighten up did he remember where he was—inside a bag. It might as well have been his coffin. Then he felt the pain, the throbbing at the back of his head that was making his skull ring. He couldn't even reach up to feel the spot—the bag was too tight. He lay still then and tried to gather his thoughts in spite of the hammering in his brain.

"Find Frank," he told himself. "That's the first thing." He listened for any signs of life around him. Then he whispered into the smothering dark, "Frank, are you there?"

He strained his ears—and heard the distant hum of an engine. A plane! He was on a plane! Then, nearer, he heard a rustling and scraping, which he assumed was Frank moving inside *his* bag.

"Frank, is that you?"

"Yeah." His brother's voice was laced with pain and confusion. "Where are you?"

"Inside a bag," Joe whispered. "And I think we're aboard a plane."

"Great," Frank responded sarcastically. "They airmailed us somewhere. Any ideas on how to get out of these things?"

Joe could hear struggling. "Keep it down," he warned. "We may have company."

Both of them listened, but all they caught was the deep *thrum* of propellers. Propellers! It must be a small plane. "If you can move at all, you should be able to get out of yours," Joe whispered. "You're more flexible than I am. I do have a knife, but I can't get to it."

Frank's head was at the bottom of the bag, and the drawstring was down near his feet. He pulled himself into a tuck and held the bag tight against the floor so it couldn't turn with him.

Moving a few inches with each turn, he was finally able to grope the top of the bag. Frank tried to force his fingers through the tiny hole to reach the knotted rope.

But he couldn't squeeze them through. He dug into his pocket and found a key, which he brought up, and began the slow process of loosening the knot.

19

"How's it going?" Joe asked after listening to Frank's deliberate breathing for a few minutes.

"I'll be done in a minute," Frank whispered. His fingers ached, but he'd managed to pry open the knot. Then he pushed open the mouth of the bag and peeked out.

They were in the cargo section of a small plane. Leading into the cockpit was an open door that let in the dull glare of an overcast day. Wisps of cloud whipped by the front window. Bundles, packages, and crates had been dumped everywhere, and they bounced and shifted as the plane cut through the cloud cover.

After crawling out of the sack, Frank untied the knot on Joe's. Silently, they moved on all fours toward the cockpit door, pausing to take cover behind crates. A large bearded man was asleep just outside the door, a parachute strapped to his back, a revolver in his lap.

Hunkering behind an open shipping case, Joe asked, "What do you think?"

"Give me a minute," Frank said, rubbing his sore head.

"I see only one chance," Joe said. "We grab the gun and hijack the plane."

Frank nodded and tried to ignore his pounding head. He straightened to take another look at their sleeping guard and glanced down into the crate in front of him. Inside was a kind of giant sea buoy with a beacon and what looked like radio equipment attached to it. Strange, he thought to himself. I've never seen anything like that.

But he didn't have time to think more about it. The man with the gun began to stir. As he moved Frank saw that he was sitting on a pile of packed parachutes.

The bearded guard startled himself awake with a snuffling snort and rubbed a hamlike fist across his eyes. His head snapped up, and he focused immediately on the empty mail sacks. Jumping up with more speed and grace than most men fifty pounds lighter, he scurried nervously around the cargo bay, searching for his escaped prisoners. He got to Frank's hiding place first.

In two moves Frank shot up and kicked out with both feet to try to knock the revolver from the goon's hand.

But his kick was off the mark, and Frank fell, landing violently on his side. The bull of a man was on him in a flash. Frank watched as the butt end of the revolver came crashing toward him. The blow only glanced off his head, but Frank still saw red and orange circles swim across his eyes as he lay stunned for a moment.

Joe gave a war whoop and swooped down on the man from his perch on a crate. But the hulk's reflexes were quick. He reached out and grabbed Joe's wrist, flipping him over on his back. Joe's head caught the full impact, and he was knocked unconscious.

Dropping the gun, the guard reached out for

both of Joe's wrists and dragged him over to the hatch. Boosting Joe up onto his hip, he held him tight against his body with one arm and released the lever on the hatch with the other.

Frank watched and, in a sudden burst of understanding, knew that the goon was planning to drop Joe from the plane as soon as the hatch was fully open.

Frank focused all his concentration, shook his head to clear it, and dove for the parachutes.

Supporting Joe against his hip, the guard continued to struggle with the door against the wind and pressure. He had it slid halfway open. Joe would be tossed out in another few seconds.

Frank slipped on the chute, snapped it closed, and pocketed the gun he had retrieved from the floor.

The goon, in one final shove, had the door open.

Frank dove for Joe just as the hulk released him into the whistling air. He caught Joe by the belt. The blast of cold had an almost instant reviving effect on Joe, and he woke up as soon as Frank snatched him. He wrenched his body around and clung to Frank's shoulders. The boys were sinking through the white puffs of cloud vapor, too insubstantial to support even a feather.

As soon as they were free of the plane Frank yanked the rip cord on his chute and tightened his grip on Joe. The air caught the silk, and the boys felt the welcome tug that broke their free fall. They drifted slowly down to a moonlike landscape.

Rocky hills covered with green lichen and moss stretched as far as the eye could see. Fifteen feet before touching down Joe hopped off, bent his knees, and landed in a tuck two feet from Frank. They were on a fairly gentle slope a few hundred yards from a narrow but swift little river. They had to be miles inland, from the wide expanse of water they had seen from the air.

After gathering up his chute, Frank tucked it under a stone. Both boys scouted around for any shelter in the barren tundra. The only sounds were the constant hiss of the wind and the water as it tumbled over the rocks in the riverbed.

Frank found a smooth, flat place at the foot of a huge rock. It was out of the wind and close to the river, so they'd have plenty to drink. Joe ran back for the parachute and, using his pocket-knife, cut it in half to make a tent. The remaining material would serve as bedding—on a mattress of moss, parachute wouldn't be a bad blanket.

"What's for breakfast?" Joe asked once their shelter was set up. He looked at his watch. It was three o'clock in the morning, and the sky was still filled with light.

"Well, you can have moss with water, or lichen with a few roots shredded on top," Frank joked. They stood for a moment, looking for a place to search out something to eat.

"Look over there," Joe said, pointing upstream. "See that bunch of bushes? We've got firewood, at least."

Frank turned to see a cluster of dead alders by the river's edge. "Great," he said. "Now all we need is something to cook."

"How about fish?" Joe smiled.

"But how are you—?"

"Wait. A little trust, please. Genius at work."

Joe whipped his belt off, cut the buckle away, then pried its pin free. He began to rub the small piece of metal back and forth until he'd sharpened it into a point. With another rock he gently hammered the pin into a hook shape.

"There you go—one grade-B, size-ten fishhook," he declared, proudly holding it up for Frank to see.

"All *riiight,*" Frank said. "Now let's tie some string to it and—uh-oh, no string."

Joe held up a finger. "It's a good thing I'm here." He yanked up some clumps of sparse grass and began braiding it into a few feet of line.

While Joe was busy, Frank hunted for bait. Among the alders he found grubs.

Joe dropped the baited hook into the stream and it quickly disappeared under the swift water.

The line twitched almost instantly. Then, in a flash, there was a fierce tug, and the line was pulled tight.

"I've got a bite," Joe yelled excitedly.

"Get him in fast," Frank called. "Don't give him time to bite the line or rub it on a rock!"

Joe walked straight back from the edge of the river, holding his hands high above his head. The fish followed and flopped onto the rocky bank—a huge, fat northern pike.

Frank scooped up the fish in his bare hands. Removing the hook, he held it up.

"Must be at least four pounds," Joe gloated, coming over for a closer look. While Frank built a fire, Joe cleaned the catch, casually tossing the guts toward the stream.

After building a little grill out of wet alder sticks, they roasted the fish quickly. The meat was moist and flavorful and hot enough to burn their fingers as they picked it apart.

Just as they were finishing, the quiet of the sunlit night was interrupted by the sound of someone splashing along the river's edge. A large brown bear.

"Got the revolver?" Joe whispered.

"In the tent," Frank said, not taking his eyes from the lumbering beast. "I'll get it." He moved quickly and silently and returned holding the gun down by his thigh. "I don't know if it'll do much damage in this case."

"You may be right." Joe kept his eyes on the bear, who continued waddling downstream toward them. "It'd probably do just enough to make him mad. Is it a grizzly?"

"Looks like it," Frank answered. "It's got that kind of silver fur around its throat." He glanced

25

at the fire. "It probably smelled the fish. Where'd you put the guts?"

"I threw them in the—" Joe stopped suddenly, staring. The fish guts had landed on a nearby rock. "Uh-oh."

"Nice going," Frank said. "Let's sneak into the tent. Maybe he'll eat the guts and go away."

They inched backward toward the tent. The bear came right up to the fish guts. In one gulp, he licked them up. Then, twitching his nose, he headed for what was left of the fish beside the fire.

"He's coming nearer," Joe whispered, eyes wide.

The bear had obviously caught Joe's and Frank's scents. Abruptly it rose up on its hind legs, throwing a shadow thirty feet long that fell like night over the boys. No one breathed. Time was frozen for a second.

Then Frank raised the gun. The movement attracted the beast, and the unnatural silence was shattered with one giant roar as the grizzly began its charge!

Chapter

4

FRANK STOOD HIS ground and, arms extended, took careful aim before squeezing off a single shot. Nothing! Only a click—the gun was jammed. The bear kept coming.

Then a second later a gunshot blast cut through the air. Frank and Joe didn't stop to think where it had come from because their eyes were still on the bear. It quit its attack, stood on its hind legs, and rolled its massive head to find the distraction. Coming up the riverbank were a man and a dog. The man had a rifle in his hands, pointed straight up. Another gunshot, and the bear whoofed once and fled.

The man waved, and the Hardys managed a quick nod of their heads. Holding his rifle casually at waist level, the man trotted toward them with the dog at his side.

"Hello!" the man greeted the boys. "You had a little scare there, eh?"

As he got closer Frank and Joe could see that he was a native Alaskan. His face was a perfect circle of copper-colored leather that had to have taken many years outdoors to acquire. Squinting in the sunlight, his shiny black-pebble eyes were surrounded by deep lines.

"I thought we were dead. Thanks," Frank said simply, and extended his hand in greeting. "Boy, were we glad to see *you*."

The man laughed and then shook his head. "Not much you can do when a bear's hungry."

"I guess not," Joe said, glancing upstream to make sure the bear had really gone. He saw only the river and the endless barren hills.

"Are you hunting?" the man asked, looking them over skeptically.

"Uh, not exactly," Frank said.

"I hope not. Not in those clothes," the stranger remarked, pointing to their sneakers. "Need some help?"

They nodded eagerly. "Guess you could say that. We don't even know where we are. We had an emergency and had to jump from our plane."

The man scanned the area without speaking. He thought he might see the wreckage of a crash. "Too bad. You both okay?" was all he said. He obviously didn't want to pry.

"Yeah, we're okay. Just a little tired. We'd like

to get to Prudhoe," Joe said. "Do you know the way?"

"No problem. I'm a hunting and fishing guide. My name's Virgil Asuluk."

Frank and Joe breathed a sigh of relief. "I'm Joe Hardy, and this is my brother, Frank."

"Pleased to meet you. This is Tanook. He's a lead dog. Very good animal." Tanook was a large, silvery husky, with the big chest and broad head characteristic of his breed. When Virgil began to walk off, Tanook sprang to his side.

They picked up their parachute and followed Virgil along the river. He explained that one of his fishing camps was at the mouth of the river. "My helicopter is there. I'll fly you back to Prudhoe."

"Helicopter?" Joe asked.

"Times have changed. We have planes and snowmobiles. But we also keep our good friends, like Tanook."

The dog barked once at his name, and a helicopter circled them lazily.

The Hardys explained why they were in Alaska as they trudged along.

"Those companies are not good," Virgil said, shaking his head when he'd heard their story. "Often they won't hire the Aleut or the Athapaskan, and we make complaints." He explained to the Hardys about the different tribes of Indian and Eskimo peoples in the north. "Sometimes you have to pay to get a job." His eyes were open wide to emphasize the shock.

"That's what our friends found out. And one got chased home, and the other one has disappeared. Now we've been kidnapped and almost killed. It looks as if it might be more serious than just kickbacks for jobs." Frank was grim as he marched along, matching his pace to Virgil's.

"Not good, not good." Virgil shook his head and paused. "You must find your friend."

An hour later they came to a small flat plain at the mouth of the river. Across the open space a dozen tethered dogs barked happily to greet their master. Strips of raw fish were hung out on large wooden racks to dry in the sun. A fishing boat lay on its side in the grass, and a red and white helicopter stood off by itself like a giant, futuristic insect.

Virgil led the Hardys to the chopper. He climbed up on the strut and put his rifle inside. Then he turned the ignition key to activate the battery. Rock music boomed out of the open door. Virgil grinned. "New speakers—put them in myself."

"Great." Joe's eyes shone. The thought of whipping through the sky on the wings of full-blast rock 'n' roll was kind of exciting.

"I have lots of tapes. You can pick what you like for the trip later." Virgil shut down the system. "But right now let's get you something warm to drink."

He led the way toward a small sod hut that had grass sprouting on its roof. Some rough wooden beams framed the door and the small windows on each side of the structure. A chimney seemed to grow out of the roof.

"Come in, come in," Virgil said, ducking through the door and gesturing for them to follow. Inside it was dark but warm and comfortable. The floor was hard-packed dirt. Hunting and trapping equipment hung on the dried mud walls, along with beautifully carved fishing spears. Six cots were stacked neatly on top of one another in one corner. Virgil went to the cast-iron stove and opened it up.

"I'll get this going a little better. Tea okay?" They both nodded.

"I bring folks here for the fishing," Virgil explained as he busied himself with the tea. "Every month in the summer I have a new group."

He chatted about his copter and the fish and game as the Hardys quietly sipped the hot, sweet tea.

Abruptly in the middle of a good fishing story Virgil stopped, his head bent toward a window and his eyes unfocused. He was listening. "Someone is coming." Frank and Joe heard nothing, but they followed Virgil outside. The dogs were all standing up and looking in the same direction. Virgil stared off into the sky.

"What are we supposed to be hearing?" Frank asked.

"A chopper—maybe more than one," Virgil said. "Maybe someone looking for you?" He looked at them intently.

Frank shrugged. "Could be," he said. He and Joe exchanged nervous glances.

"I hear it now," Frank said. They watched as Virgil lifted his arm to the sky.

"There they are, three of them!"

The dogs began to whimper with excitement, but Virgil didn't seem to notice. He kept his eyes on the choppers.

"Are they coming here?" Joe asked.

"Don't know," Virgil said, shading his eyes. "Looks like they're flying a search pattern. They're moving slow and low to the ground."

The distinctive shuddering *whirr* of helicopter rotors grew louder and louder. The choppers were zigzagging back and forth, but Frank realized they were probably following the path of the river.

"Hmm," Virgil said, slightly surprised. "I think I recognize them." He squinted into the sun. "Yes—North Slope Supply. I thought they went out of business."

"What are they?" Joe asked.

"A small company," Virgil replied, still keeping his head raised to the approaching craft. "Small construction projects—they work for larger companies as subcontractors."

Frank and Joe nodded. The choppers must have noticed the camp, since they were coming toward them. The hovering machines couldn't have been more than a hundred feet above the ground.

Frank and Joe could see the North Slope Supply logo emblazoned across the sides of all three copters. The noise became almost unbearable as the choppers came closer. The wind from the whirling blades felt hard and unpleasant against their faces.

When the copters were about forty feet above the ground, the side door on one of them slid open abruptly. A man stood framed against the interior darkness. In his hands was a submachine gun with a string of shiny brass cartridge cases flying from the chamber.

Flaming death was spitting from the gun's muzzle, and it was aimed at the boys and Virgil.

Chapter

5

FRANK AND JOE lunged directly under the hovering chopper to get out of the line of fire. Virgil sprinted for the sod house, zigzagging across the open space. Unable to take aim at the Hardys, the man in the chopper followed Virgil with his heavy weapon.

His bullets stitched the earth, but because of the position of the chopper and Virgil's quick and erratic movements a hit was impossible. The Hardys could hear the gunner yelling at the pilot to spin the copter around.

As the bird began its turn Joe pointed to the fishing boat lying on its side. They dashed from under the shadow of the chopper, ducking and weaving as Virgil had. Halfway to the boat they were hit with clods of earth as bullets ripped up the ground behind them. The chopper was zeroing in—and fast. The sound of the copter got louder, and they could feel the shadow on their backs.

"Hit the dirt," Joe yelled. They dove apart, belly-flopping on the ground and rolling away as a burst of fire marched between them. The chopper overshot, and they sprang the last few yards to the cover of the fishing boat.

Catching their breath, they peered around the craft to see what was happening. The choppers must have been talking to one another by radio. The machine gun was silent as the chopper hovered nearby; the other two were hovering out of firing range.

Suddenly the copter on the attack flashed toward the sod hut. Frank and Joe saw Virgil running around to the back of the house with a fishing spear in his hand. The attack chopper was stalking him.

Keeping the house between himself and the enemy above, Virgil was playing a cat-and-mouse game with the machine gunner. He ran, luring the chopper this way and that. Then he'd duck inside or leap through a window just as the gunner must have thought he had a clear shot. Once Virgil disappeared, the pilot had to guess where he'd jump out next and maneuver the helicopter into position.

Virgil burst through a window and rolled across the ground with a spear.

The chopper was caught out of position, and

Virgil jumped up and ran to its blind side. In a split second he snapped the spear forward. The razor-sharp projectile left his hand with the force of a missile and pierced the fiberglass housing on the chopper's engine, burying itself in the gearbox.

At first it seemed as if the blow had had no effect on the hovering craft. The gunner continued blasting the sides and roof of the hut as Virgil dived around it for cover. Then the chopper began spinning in an erratic bobbing and weaving pattern. It limped off a safe distance and landed.

But as soon as it moved off another copter started toward them. "Let's run for the hut," Joe suggested.

"Too chancy," Frank replied. "They know we aren't armed, so they won't be cautious."

Suddenly Virgil burst out of his house, zigzagging toward his dogs. He ran by each one and unhooked it from its tether. The new chopper didn't pay much attention. It hovered in front of the fishing boat as Virgil sprinted back to the house.

"We've got to think of something," Joe said. "They'll pick us off like fish in a barrel." He ducked back behind the boat, knocking his head on a large wooden box mounted in the bow of the boat. The lid fell open, and a jumble of marine equipment burst out—lines, nets, a can of engine oil, and a flare gun with flares.

"Is this what I think it is?" Joe asked, showing it to Frank.

"Uh-huh. Does it work?"

"We'll soon find out."

Joe peered over the edge of the boat. The chopper's pilot and passenger were on the ground now, moving toward the sod hut. Only the passenger had a gun, and he was obviously more concerned with Virgil and his possible stash of weapons than with the boys.

Taking aim, Joe launched a flare into the open door of the sitting chopper. It exploded inside the enclosed space like a bomb. Blinding light and thick smoke came belching out. The two men whirled around at the sneak attack and began to back away, pointing their weapons first at the house, then at the boat.

The last chopper played it safe. Since it was the only bird able to fly, its pilot put down at a safe distance. The one crew member jumped out and went running to help his friends. As he was crossing the open space Virgil shouted something from the door of the hut.

His sled dogs suddenly sprang to life, charging the crewmen.

And at the same time a huge explosion erupted from the helicopter with the flare burning in it. Flames had reached the fuel tank, and the whole chopper was being blown to pieces.

"Let's go!" Joe shouted. He and Frank leapt out from behind the boat. Virgil had the same idea. With the enemy momentarily startled and pinned down by the dogs, they made a run for Virgil's chopper, Tanook leading the way.

Gunshots cracked as they dodged across the clearing, but there was so much smoke in the air there was little danger of being hit. They clambered into the helicopter and took off, rising above the dark, billowing clouds. Tanook was whimpering in the back as they rose from the ground.

"Will the dogs be all right?" Frank asked.

"No one in Alaska will shoot a dog," Virgil said. He glanced down at the clearing to make sure what he said was true. Frank and Joe looked down, too. They could see the enemy running for the one good chopper. The dogs pursued them, barking and growling, but they stopped short of attacking.

Virgil headed for Prudhoe. Even at some distance, they could still see the plume of smoke rising from the burning chopper.

"We'll go in over the mountains," Virgil was saying. "Who knows how fast their copter is."

They looked back. The last North Slope helicopter was in the air and coming after them. It was bigger than Virgil's, and probably faster.

"What'll we do if they catch up with us?" Frank asked.

Virgil shrugged. "First try to lose them. If we can't do that, then we'll worry about being caught." He turned the copter abruptly and began to drop closer to the ground.

"I know these valleys," he said. "If we can get behind a mountain, we can hide from them, put down, and disguise the chopper. They may be faster, but we're quicker. There's a difference."

Virgil looked grim, but he couldn't resist turning on the stereo. A heavy rock beat came thudding dramatically from the speakers, drowning out the sound from the engines and rotor. Joe turned to Frank, grinning. "Music to escape by," he mouthed. It was like a movie soundtrack. There they were, swooping across the Brooks Range, pursued by a helicopter while listening to the same music they'd heard at Lisa Shannon's party.

"This is something else," Joe cried, taking in the scenery and keeping an eye on the approaching chopper. "Virgil, they're gaining on us."

"Not much I can do," Virgil responded. He craned his neck around to see the enemy. When he realized how close they were, he hung a hard right and dropped into a narrow valley.

"Better try it now," he said. But the North Slope chopper was right behind them and seemed to have no trouble keeping up.

Suddenly Virgil leaned forward and began to fiddle with the throttle controls. He tapped the gauges, muttering to himself.

"What's wrong?" Frank asked.

"Doesn't feel good," he said, adjusting two

more knobs. "It's like we're running out of fuel, but that's not possible. I filled it up this morning."

Frank and Joe felt helpless.

"No," Virgil said grimly. "Something's definitely wrong. We're losing altitude, and the fuel is way down." The engine skipped and sputtered. Joe leaned back in his seat and tried to see the enemy. Little drops of moisture appeared on the window next to him.

"Hey, it's raining," he said, tapping on the glass. But it didn't make any sense. The sun was out. There wasn't any moisture on any of the other windows.

The engine began to cough more and more. Joe looked up to see what was happening. Not a cloud in the sky. What he did see was a stream of fuel pouring out of a bullet hole in their gas tank.

"We've got a leak," he said over the sound of the music, which must have masked the gunshots. "It's coming down my side."

As Virgil glanced over to see the growing stream roll down the window, the engine stopped for a good five seconds. The music shut down, and the chopper began to fall like a stone.

Chapter

6

THE SUDDEN SILENCE was eerie. No music, no rotor. Just the click of the engine ticking down as it cooled. The plunge to the earth felt the same as if they'd been on a good roller coaster—but a lot less fun.

"Hold on," Virgil said calmly. He flipped a switch and began to pull on a knob on the control panel. "Let's hope this works." Virgil's face was tense as he turned the ignition off and then back on again.

"What are you doing?" Joe asked, his voice tight.

"Got a reserve tank," Virgil explained. "Never use it. Don't know if it's full or how the line is."

The starter cranked over and over, but the engine only coughed and died. The ground came closer and closer. They were over a forest in the middle of a deep valley. Joe was already picking out their crash site as Virgil cranked the starter once again.

"Do you have any chutes?" Frank asked.

"Nope." Virgil had already considered the alternative of jumping and dismissed it.

Then, with faint rumblings and stirrings, the engine suddenly began to turn over. "She's catching." Virgil smiled. "Feel her? There she goes!"

Frank and Joe felt the sudden surge of power as the blades bit into the air and lifted the chopper out of her death plunge. They were down low enough to watch treetop branches wave in the sudden blast of air.

"We'll have to put down real soon. There's not much in this little tank, and once it goes, that's it." Virgil scanned the area for a place to land in the dense forest below.

Frank's mind was churning. How would they get out of this and get back to Prudhoe? They had to find Scott, bring him home if they could. Instead, they were in the middle of nowhere, on the run in a damaged helicopter, pursued by unknown thugs dead set on killing them. It was starting to make him mad.

He looked up. "I've got an idea. Virgil—do you have any rope? Any tools aboard?"

Virgil nodded. "In the back. There's a big coil of rope and a complete tool chest. Why?"

"Find a clearing, a small clearing."

Virgil and Joe looked over at him.

"What are you talking about?" Joe burst out. "That's what we're doing!"

"I mean a *really* small clearing, just big enough for two choppers—and one trap."

"You'd better talk fast," Joe said.

Quickly Frank described what he had in mind. Virgil and Joe listened intently. Then Virgil began to grin.

"Sounds like it's worth a try. Let's go." He swung the chopper around and headed for what Joe pointed out as the only good place to land. The North Slope chopper was still following, but at a safe distance. Maybe its occupants feared some kind of trick.

Virgil put the bird down as close to the trees as he could, the rotor blades whirling only inches from branches. To the left, only a slightly larger space remained. There was no place else for the other chopper to land.

"Let's go," Frank called. "We don't have much time. Don't let them see what we're up to."

He grabbed the tool chest, throwing his parka over it to conceal it from their enemies. Joe had the coil of rope under his jacket.

"Come on, into the woods," Frank urged them. Virgil and Joe ducked into the cover of the trees.

"What's first?" Virgil asked, peering up at the North Shore copter through the branches.

"Pick a tree on the other side of the clearing and get a rope around the top of it. Then we make a cut in the trunk with the saw."

"Right!" Joe burst out into the clearing.

"Get back!" Frank yelled.

Joe plunged back under the canopy of leaves. "What's the matter?"

"Don't let them see you," Frank said as he started pushing his way around the perimeter of the clearing. "We want them to think we've made a run for it."

"This looks like a good one," Virgil said, tapping a tall tree on the opposite side of the tiny meadow.

"Too tall," Frank responded, staring up at the top. "It would land on our chopper, too."

"How about this one?" Joe called out, standing next to a slender, dark-barked tree a few yards in from the edge of the clearing.

"That's better," Frank said. "Looks just the right height. And the fact that it's in from the edge is good. Not so obvious. Can you climb it, Joe?"

With the rope wrapped diagonally around his torso, he began to shinny up the tree trunk.

"How high do you think we should put it?" he called down.

"That's about right—right now," Frank yelled up.

Joe slipped the rope off and tied it snugly around the trunk. He dropped the end of the rope to the ground and came down as easily as he'd gone up.

"Okay. Now let's cut a *V* on the side opposite the direction of the fall," Frank said. Grabbing one end of the saw, he and Virgil removed a wedge from the back of the tree. The upper half of the tree was now standing on a quarter of its trunk.

They could hear the enemy chopper circling down closer. Virgil looked up. "They've been trying to figure out what we're up to," Virgil said. "I guess they've decided we ran. Now they have to come down to find out which way."

"Let's get this thing finished," Frank said.

Taking the end of the rope, he trailed it along behind him as he headed back to the other side of the clearing. It wasn't easy keeping the rope clean and yet remaining hidden in the trees. Joe and Virgil followed.

"Okay, Joe. Loop it through a branch on this side, and then let it go slack. The rope has to lie flat. We don't want them to see it." Joe went up with the rope and was back in a flash.

"Okay, all set!" he said.

They positioned themselves at the end of the rope. The North Slope chopper hovered just forty feet over the clearing. They were within easy firing range. The Hardys and Virgil could see the machine gunner and two friends with revolvers peering around the edge of the open door.

"This is it," Joe said.

As the chopper lowered itself into the final fifteen feet of descent, Frank gave the signal. They pulled the rope tight, lashing it firmly around the trunk of the tree. The enemy pilot never saw it. But the chopper certainly felt it.

The rope snapped up from the ground, right under the helicopter's belly. It caught one of the wheel struts, making the copter tilt. That put more weight on the rope, and the cut tree toppled, knocking the helicopter out of the air. The chopper smashed to the ground, one of its rotor blades flying off with a metallic *twang*.

Frank and Joe ran up to the open door of the helicopter. Five men lay piled in a heap. All were alive but unconscious. Joe gathered up the guns and threw them into Virgil's chopper. Frank checked the copter's pilot, who was out cold but breathing. His last act had been to cut off the engine before crashing.

"Okay," Frank said, jumping down. "Let's patch our fuel tank and siphon their gas off. These guys'll be all right."

Virgil was already at work on the fuel tank. Once he gave the okay, Joe used a length of rubber hose to suck the fuel out of the North Slope chopper and direct it into Virgil's.

"Let's hope the patch holds," Virgil said over the noise of the engine as it lifted them up over the mountains. They didn't have to worry—the tank held all the way to Prudhoe.

Virgil dropped them on the outskirts of town before he flew off to check on his dogs.

"Don't worry," he yelled out as the chopper lifted off. "I'm with you—and I've got friends." As he waved Tanook barked a goodbye from the seat next to him.

Frank and Joe changed motels after picking up their things. The walls in the old room had been repaired, covering up any sign of a forced entry. It was obvious the motel management had been paid off.

"So, what do you think?" Frank asked. "Do we march into North Slope Supply and ask why they tried to kill us?"

"No," Joe answered, checking out the walls in the new motel. "But we do have to go there and snoop around. They must have a very good reason for trying to get rid of us."

"Let me try something," said Frank, picking up the phone. "Could I have a number for Scott Sanders, please?"

"No such listing in Prudhoe," he mouthed to Joe. "Then could I have the number for North Slope Supply?" He dialed the number and got through to North Slope.

When he asked for Scott Sanders, the company said they had no record of an employee with that name.

"There has to be a connection," Joe said. "We go to Trans-Yukon, Hammond gets upset. Cindy

47

warns us, but we still get kidnapped and almost killed. Then, when we escape, North Slope comes after us with half an army. They've got to be in on it.''

"In on what?" Frank asked, throwing up his hands.

"I don't know. But I'm beginning to suspect Scott might be able to tell us.''

The boys stood outside the gate of North Slope Supply as the employees trooped out at closing time. They were showing their photograph of Scott and asking if anyone knew him. Some said he looked familiar, but not one person could identify him.

When the men had all driven away, the gate guards beckoned the Hardys over.

"Can we help you boys?" a guard with a beefy, friendly face asked. His big belly strained over his gunbelt.

"Maybe," Frank said. "We're looking for a friend of ours. We thought he worked here, but we haven't been able to find him." He held up the picture for the guard to see.

"No, don't think so," the fat guard said. "How about you, Smitty? Recognize this face?"

He handed the picture to the other guard, who shook his head, but Frank noticed that his eyes continued to glare at the picture.

"Tell you what," said the first guard. "Come

on into the guard house and we'll look up his name on the computer.''

''Great! Thanks a lot,'' Joe said. They stepped into the small booth. Two chairs and a built-in table, with a computer and phone, filled most of one wall. Joe was surprised to see submachine guns hanging on the wall.

''What was that name?''

''Scott Sanders,'' Joe said.

The heavy guard punched a few buttons on the computer, and Frank knew immediately that he was bluffing. Before he could say anything, Smitty moved up behind them to block the door, his hand on the butt of his revolver.

''Okay, boys. How about telling us what you're really here for?''

Chapter

7

THE FAT GUARD whirled around and slapped a hamlike fist into his open palm. "Answer the man!" he snarled.

"We told you the truth," Joe said, trapped between the two guards. "We're looking for our friend Scott Sanders."

"Yeah? What else?" It seemed Fatso was taking over the interrogation.

"Nothing else. We just want to make sure he's all right."

"You expect us to believe that? Two kids come all the way to Alaska—"

"How do you know about us?" Frank asked.

"Never mind. We know. What are your names?"

"I'm Frank Hardy, this is my brother Joe, and

we're friends of Scott Sanders. Does he work here? That's all we want to know.''

Fatso laughed. "A lot of people work here, kid. And it's none of your business what their names are. Especially when you're trespassing.''

"How can we be trespassing when you invited us in?" Joe asked as innocently as possible.

The guard's face tightened and became mask-like. "It's time,'' he said, nodding to Smitty.

Joe was ready and ducked when Smitty swung. While the guard was off balance, he landed a solid blow to Smitty's solar plexus. The shocked guard doubled over with a gasp. But when Joe moved in to follow it up, Smitty rapped a night-stick across Joe's knee.

The sudden pain made Joe totter, and Smitty threw the stick around Joe's throat. Joe swung his elbows wide and rammed them into Smitty's stomach. *Whoosh!* The air rushed out of him. Joe whirled around and landed one punch that reduced Smitty to an unconscious heap on the floor.

While Smitty was trying to dispose of Joe, Fatso had gone for his gun.

Frank snapped off a karate kick to jar the gun out of the guard's hand just as it cleared the holster. The kick landed perfectly, ramming the revolver into Fatso's hip. But then the guard raised the gun to aim it point-blank at Frank.

Frank couldn't believe the man was still holding the gun after the kick he'd delivered.

But before Fatso could pull the trigger, Joe was

flying across the room and landing spread-eagle on top of the man. His gun jerked up and discharged into the ceiling. The thunder continued to bounce off the walls for several seconds. Joe grabbed the downed man's wrist and pried the gun out of his hands. A quick chop to his fleshy jaw and Fatso was out cold.

"I thought I was a goner," Frank said. "Thanks."

"It all evens out," Joe said with a quick grin. "Let's tie these bozos up. I want to get inside and see what's going on."

They handcuffed the guards, then cut the phone wires. After borrowing their guns, the boys walked through the main gate to North Slope Supply and closed it after them.

"Think anybody's here?" Joe asked.

"Doesn't look like it," Frank whispered, looking around the empty yard.

North Slope Supply consisted of a collection of small buildings surrounded by a chain-link fence. Two Quonset huts stood side by side along the western edge of the compound. A concrete bunker and a cluster of old sheds were scattered on the eastern side. In the middle of the lot stood a modern, one-story office building, its shiny white walls in direct contrast to the tired buildings around it. Long rectangular windows of tinted glass started at ground level and ran up to the roof. The entire place was deserted.

"It *is* after hours," Frank muttered, trying to convince himself that everything was normal.

"Let's check out one of these huts," Joe said.

They headed across the hard-packed dirt and ducked into the unlocked door of the first hut. It was hot inside. The air smelled of mildew, as though wet cardboard had been decaying there for years.

"Nothing here," Frank said. "This is weird. The company is called North Slope *Supply*, but there aren't any supplies."

"It is spooky," Joe agreed. "This is a company that can afford three helicopters, and their plant looks like it could barely buy three wheelbarrows."

"Come on. Let's check out the rest." They walked through the Quonset hut and out the other end. Continuing through the second hut, which was also empty, they came to the concrete bunker. This door was bolted shut.

Joe found a rusty iron bar and pried the bolt off the door. Frank hesitated at the entrance, looking behind him. "I have the feeling we're being watched," he said.

Joe shrugged. "From where? I haven't even seen a squirrel." He stepped into the bunker, and into pitch-dark. But as his eyes adjusted, he could make out a dim shape. "There's something over there," he said.

"What is it?" Frank had his back to the room, still scanning the quiet yard.

"I can't really tell—it looks like some kind of buoy."

Frank wrinkled his brow. A buoy? Where had he seen a buoy recently?

Joe came out. "Nothing else." He closed the door, leaving the bolt hanging.

Frank continued to mull over the strange emptiness of the place. "I can't believe there's nothing here. No equipment, no office supplies, no uniforms, no files—no nothing!"

"I don't see why it's so strange. Look, the office building is new. Maybe when it was built they moved everything in there."

"I can't see them storing backhoes, bulldozers, and graders in there." Frank shook his head. "It looks like this is a dummy company. But whose dummy?"

"Maybe it's Hammond's," Joe suggested. "Cindy heard him talking about getting rid of us, so I think we can assume that he sent the guys to mail us into the wilderness, right?"

"I'm with you."

"But when we escaped, who came looking for us?"

Frank nodded. "North Slope! So Trans-Yukon and North Slope might be connected somehow." He frowned. "But remember in the hut how Virgil was surprised North Slope was still around? Maybe they went bankrupt and sold off their equipment—choppers and all. That would explain all this empty storage space."

"But it wouldn't explain how the guys at the gate knew us." Joe headed for the office building. "What I want to know is, where does Scott fit in?"

"Think," said Frank. "The only thing we've said to these people is that we want to find Scott. And they keep trying to kill us. Somehow we represent a big threat to them—or Scott does."

They reached the side of the building. Standing between two long windows, Joe leaned over and tried to peer inside.

"Can't see a thing. The glass is tinted," he said.

Frank joined him, cupping his hands around his eyes as he pressed his face against the glass.

"You can see a little if you block out the light. I think . . . yeah, I do see someone in there."

"Does he look like that picture of Scott?" Joe asked.

Frank looked again. The figure was seated at a desk in profile. He seemed to be assembling some kind of electronic device. "Kind of. It could be him."

He grabbed Joe's arm before he could bang on the window. "Scott doesn't know who we are. And we don't know if he's alone."

"There's only one way to find out," Joe suggested. "Let's go in."

"Are you nuts?" Frank whispered. "These guys have tried to kill us at least three times, and you want to walk right into their nest?"

"How else are we going to talk to Scott? If that's him, it's worth a try."

Against his better judgment, Frank agreed. Stealing around the corner, they approached the thick glass door. Joe tested it, and it opened easily. He motioned for Frank to follow him in. Holding a gun ready, they walked cautiously into a brightly lit corridor.

"I don't see any security cameras, do you?" Joe asked.

"No, but they could be hidden. I don't like this, Joe. It's too easy."

"Well, I'm sorry I couldn't make it any harder," Joe said. "Come on. He's in there." He pointed to a door at the end of the hall.

About ten feet from the door they heard a strange hissing sound. They stopped. Nothing. "Heating system, I guess," Joe whispered.

A few more steps and they tasted something in their mouths—a strange tang. "Gas!" Frank yelled.

They tried to run back down the hall to get outside, but their legs became leaden. They staggered, and then their legs turned to rubber.

Frank watched the floor swim up to meet his eyes. Then there was nothing but darkness.

Chapter

8

JOE HARDY STRUGGLED to consciousness and out of his drugged sleep. The muscles he needed to open his eyes weren't able to do their job. Even when he did force his eyes open, he felt as if he were looking at the world from somewhere in the back of his head.

He reached up to rub his eyes, but his hands wouldn't move. At first he thought that, like his eyes, they were just heavy and taking their time to wake up. Then the awful realization dawned that he was strapped down—his wrists, chest, and ankles all immobilized.

With horror he decided he was strapped to an electric chair. There were wires attached to his arms, and other wires emerged from under his shirt.

Straining against the leather straps, he only

exhausted himself pulling against them. It was hopeless. Whoever had tied him up had done a professional job. He couldn't even remember what had happened to him; his mind couldn't focus on a single event.

"Mr. Hardy. I see you're with us again. How was your little nap?"

Joe tried to focus and eventually saw a short, blond man framed in a doorway. He was wearing a business suit and carrying a sheaf of papers under his arm.

"Where am I?" Joe asked. He didn't recognize the man or the room he was in. Maybe he was dreaming, he decided. None of this made sense.

"You are on the property of North Slope Supply," the man said gently. "How are you feeling?"

"Not good," Joe responded. "What happened?"

"Perhaps I should ask you the same question."

What *had* happened? Then slowly it dawned on him. They'd been stealing down the hallway on their way to see Scott, when—

"I can't really remember," he lied, playing for time.

The blond man laughed. "Let *me* refresh your memory. You were sneaking along one of our hallways last night, and you triggered one of our security mechanisms. Do you remember now?"

Joe pretended to try to remember. "Oh, yes,"

he said, as if it were a great relief to know what had happened to him. "Who are you?"

"My name is Sandy White. I'm president of North Slope Supply. I'm sorry I can't shake your hand." Joe glanced at the man's face to see if he was toying with him. But White merely smiled, and Joe couldn't read the cryptic smile.

"Why do you have me tied up like this?" Joe demanded, staring the man right in the eye.

"Why were you trespassing on the grounds of my company?"

"We—I was looking for a friend of mine." Joe changed the *we* quickly. In case Frank had gotten away, he didn't want to incriminate him.

"Who might that be?"

Joe had to think fast. By now, the guards must have come to and told their boss whom he and his brother were looking for.

"I don't think I have to tell you that," Joe told the man.

"You're right," Sandy White said, standing in front of Joe's chair and staring down at him. "You were looking for someone named Scott, weren't you?"

Joe glared at him. "Then why did you ask? What are all these wires for?"

Sandy White dropped his papers on a table and slipped his hands into his pockets, leaning back against the table. "Why don't you tell me what you know about North Slope," he coaxed, examining the shine on his shoes.

"I don't know anything," Joe said. "All I know is that Scott worked for Trans-Yukon. They say he doesn't work there now. Maybe he went to work for North Slope. All I'm doing is trying to find him."

"Are you aware that North Slope does top-secret work for the government?"

Joe rested his head against the chair back. "Really? Does that give you license to kidnap people and try to kill them?"

White chuckled. "The powers of government can run pretty far. And I have big plans."

"So what are you saying? That Scott's working for the government?" Joe kept staring at the older man, trying to get any clue from his reactions.

"I didn't say that. As a matter of fact, I don't think I've ever heard of this Scott person."

This guy was giving absolutely nothing away. Joe wished that Frank was around. He squirmed against his straps.

"So you don't know anything about North Slope?" White continued.

"Nothing, but I'm learning."

"So you are," White said mildly. "You may learn a few more things shortly."

"I think I know more than I want to already," Joe told him.

"I wouldn't say that, if I were you," White said. "You asked what the wires were for."

Joe looked down again. He saw now that the wires ran across the floor and into a hole in the wall. A tinted glass panel was framed into the wall at window height just above the hole.

"I'm curious why you've been so persistent," White remarked. "You've had to overcome pretty tough obstacles so far."

"I have to keep trying," Joe said flatly.

"You don't represent any larger organization?"

"Me? No. I told you—I'm only looking for my friend."

"I see." White paused. "I'll tell you what I'm going to do. You know what a polygraph is, don't you?"

Joe nodded. "Of course. It's a lie detector."

"That's correct. The wires attached to you right now are hooked up to a polygraph machine in the next room. I'm going to turn it on, and then I'm going to ask you a few questions. Is that all right with you?"

"I don't think I'm in a position to refuse," Joe said, but his words were aimed at Sandy White's back. The man hadn't even waited for an answer.

White paused just inside the doorway and rotated his body to face Joe again. "Be back in a moment." He gave Joe another enigmatic smile. Joe wondered what kind of guy would stick someone in a torture chamber and then tell him to have a nice day.

Joe's mind was racing. What was he going to do? He really didn't know anything. Maybe that makes it better. I'll just tell the truth, he decided.

Who knows? Maybe I can even pick up some info from the questions they ask. I just wish Frank were around.

The door opened, and White returned with the polygraph machine on a little cart.

"Sorry to keep you waiting," he apologized. But his next words turned that politeness on its head. "Here are the ground rules. I ask the questions, you answer them. If you don't answer them, or if the machine shows you're not being truthful, I'll kill you. Is that clear?"

Joe took a deep breath and nodded. White's true colors were finally revealed.

"Fine. Shall we begin?"

"My time is yours."

"What's your name?"

"Joe Hardy."

White watched the machine as a mechanical arm swung a pen point over a rolling sheet of paper.

"You didn't think I'd lie about my own name, did you?"

White stared. "How old are you?"

"Seventeen."

"Where are you from?"

"Bayport. It's a town—"

"Do you have any brothers or sisters?" White cut in.

"Yes. One brother."

"What's his name?"

"Frank Hardy."

"What does your father do?"

Joe stopped. He'd been spitting back the answers as quickly as he was questioned, but this one caught him off guard. He tried to mask his hesitation with a cough.

"Sorry, I got a tickle in my throat."

"Don't bother." White pointed to a big loop on the paper where the needle and pen had swung wildly. "You know this machine doesn't say whether you're telling the truth. It measures stress—heartbeat, breathing rate, muscle tension—even how much you sweat. I can see you had a big reaction to that question. Let me ask it again. What does your father do?"

"He's retired."

"I see. Retired from what?"

"Retired from public service. He worked for the City of New York."

White leaned forward and stared at the needle of the polygraph. He let out a stream of air as if he were disappointed.

"Mr. Hardy," he began. "Your life is hanging by the proverbial thread. It is obvious to the machine and myself that you're trying to hide something. If you won't tell me, I'll have to up the ante. You see, it's *very* important to me to find out what you know."

He got up and went outside. Almost instantly the door reopened, and White reentered, wheeling a gurney, and on the gurney was Frank. His mouth was taped shut, and wires from some kind of machine were attached to his stomach.

White took those wires and attached them to the polygraph. Then he turned to Joe.

"I have just added a small electrode to this machine. Your brother has a substantial amount of plastic explosive attached to his stomach. If the polygraph needle jumps to the electrode, it will detonate the plastique.

"Of course, the explosion will kill him." White turned the corners of his mouth up in a thin-lipped grimace. "Shall we begin again?"

Chapter

9

"WAIT A MINUTE!" Joe yelled.

"I would suggest that you remain as calm as possible, Mr. Hardy. I see by the needle you are getting upset."

"Upset? Of course I'm upset. You've got my brother wired up like—like a human bomb!"

"But *you're* the detonator. Just answer the questions honestly, Mr. Hardy, and no harm will come to your brother."

Joe could see the wide sweeps the polygraph needle was making. He tried to calm down, but he couldn't stop his heart from pounding. Forcing his eyes away from the machine, he looked over at Frank. Frank's eyes were calm.

"That's better," White said soothingly. "The more you surrender, the easier this will be."

Joe exhaled in a long hiss. If he could just stay

calm and answer the questions, maybe he could figure a way out of this situation.

He remembered some of Frank's karate exercises—those to make his mind a blank. He concentrated on deep, regular breathing.

"I'll begin again," White said, drawing up a chair and placing it near the machine. "What brings you to Alaska?"

Joe stared straight ahead and spoke in a quiet voice. "We're here to find Scott and bring him home if he's in trouble."

"What makes you think this is a job for you?"

"My brother and I have done this kind of thing before." Joe felt angry that he had to spill his guts, but he forced the anger down.

"What kind of thing?" White asked, obviously pleased that he was getting somewhere.

"We've done some rescue missions and undercover work," he said.

White seemed to be amused. "For whom?"

Easy breathing—keep your mind blank, Joe told himself. He did *not* want to answer this question. "To help friends—"

"And?" White said, watching as the needle headed for the contact point.

"And for a government agency." Joe's words came out in a rush.

"Which agency?" White was pretending to have all the patience in the world.

"The Network. We've only worked indirectly—they'd never admit they knew us," Joe said.

"Don't worry, Mr. Hardy. I won't ask them for references."

Joe glanced over at Frank, who nodded his head slightly. His eyes seemed to say that Joe was doing the right thing.

"Tell me what you know about Trans-Yukon Mining," White continued.

"Only what our friend Doug told us."

"What did Doug tell you?"

"That they had a contract to work on the pipeline and some of the managers were taking bribes."

"Did he tell you what the bribes were for?"

"He didn't know, but maybe they were buying people jobs."

"Who was buying jobs?" White asked quickly.

"Doug didn't know," Joe responded.

"Do *you* know?"

"No, I don't," Joe said emphatically.

White paused. "Well . . . the polygraph says you're not lying. But I'm not so sure."

The sound of human voices drifted into the room. White glanced up and moved quickly to the door, opening it a crack. Men were shouting outside. White slipped out without saying a word.

"Frank, are you okay?" Joe was trying to keep his breathing steady and his mind empty.

Frank nodded.

"Is that a real bomb?" Joe couldn't force himself to look at the lump on Frank's stomach.

Frank nodded again. Joe closed his eyes and tried to smother the panic that had risen, sour-tasting, to his mouth. How much longer could this go on? What would happen when they were done? Would White dare to let them go?

Dimly Joe and Frank heard a now-familiar sound—the *whirr* of a helicopter. What was going on?

After a loud crash the door flew open. The needle swerved so wildly Joe didn't dare look. But when Frank began mumbling through his gag, his eyes wide with relief, Joe turned to see Virgil and Tanook in the doorway.

"I thought I'd find you in here," Virgil said. "Are you all right?"

Frank nodded his head, which was all he could do. Joe spoke as if he were in a trance.

"We're fine, Virgil, but there's a guy who'll be back any second. Please hurry." Joe was barely whispering.

Virgil looked hard at Joe. "What's wrong with your voice? Have they given you medicine?"

Joe breathed out very loudly. "I'm wired to this machine—"

Virgil nodded. "They were asking you questions to see if you tell the truth—"

"But it's also wired to a bomb on Frank's stomach. If the needle jumps too high, the bomb will explode.'' Joe's voice was hardly louder than a sigh.

Virgil could barely understand what Joe was saying. "What? Frank is taking the test, too? With a bomb on his stomach?"

Joe closed his eyes. He couldn't afford to get frustrated. "It's no test. If I get upset or excited, the machine will set off his bomb. Do you understand?"

Virgil looked from the bomb to the polygraph. "That bomb—Frank—you *had* to tell the truth!"

Joe nodded. "Right. Now please cut these wires and get us out of here."

Virgil went to the polygraph and tore out the wires. He unstrapped Joe, who ripped the wires off his own body while Virgil removed the bomb from Frank. They both helped get the tape off Frank's face.

"I'd have been here sooner," Virgil said as he went to work on the tape, "but I had to take care of the dogs, and then round up my friends. I thought there would be more trouble—and I guessed you'd head here and straight into it."

Frank was finally free from all the tape. "Let's get out of here before that creep comes back," he exclaimed, rubbing his face with both hands.

"First we've got to look for Scott," Joe said.

"No," said Virgil. "There's no one else here. I checked. Follow me!" Virgil ran to the door and peered out. "No one."

They tore down a long corridor to the front of

the building, where they heard Virgil's friends shouting at the front gate about North Slope being unfair to workers. "That drew all the guards," Virgil said. "One of my friends will bring the chopper in. Stay low."

They crouched at the side of the building, out of sight of the guards and White. Virgil pulled a small walkie-talkie from his jacket and called in the chopper. In less than two minutes it dropped in, low and fast.

When the chopper was ten feet off the ground, they sprang up and sprinted in a zigzag pattern for its open door.

The noise of the blades whipping overhead was deafening, but even it wasn't loud enough to drown out the sound of gunfire. They dove through the door headfirst.

Frank was the last one in, and as he landed the helicopter lurched. His kneecap felt shattered. The pain sent him rolling across the floor as the chopper tilted up into the dust-filled sky.

Virgil and Joe examined the damage to Frank's knee. His jeans were torn, and a mean-looking gash cut a line down his entire kneecap.

"It's not a bullet wound," Joe said. "You must have smacked your knee on the edge of the chopper as you dove in."

Frank held his leg. "This definitely has not been one of my better days."

"Take it easy," Joe said. "We'll have you fixed up in no time."

Virgil dressed the wound as the pilot headed for a hunting camp in the mountains. "You'll have to keep the leg straight for a couple of days, but it'll be all right," he said.

That night, after dropping off Virgil's friend, they sat around the fire after dinner to talk. Even though the night sky was light, the air was considerably cooler than in the day. The warmth of the flames soothed them.

"I think we've got to jump on this right now," Joe insisted. "Sandy White may think we represent the Network, and he may try to speed up his plans now."

"Well, I'm not going to be much help," Frank said, looking at his outstretched leg. "And you may think I'm crazy, but I don't think the North Slope compound is where the action is."

"What do you mean?" Joe asked.

"Well, for one thing, there were so few men there. My hunch is, White's got another base of operations, and I think it's north of here."

"North? There's only ocean north of here!" Joe exclaimed.

"Well, maybe his troops are on the ocean."

"But why north?"

"It's a matter of buoys," was all Frank offered. Frank shifted, trying to make his leg more comfortable. "It also seems evident to me that he's involved with Hammond at Trans-Yukon. Did you notice how he knew who Doug was?"

71

"Right," Joe said, remembering. "He didn't ask who Doug was when I mentioned him."

"Well, that's one thing that needs checking out at Prudhoe. I think I'll stay up here. I've got this crazy hunch about a boat or something."

"I was planning to go fishing soon," Virgil said. "Might as well go tomorrow. We can check out the immediate area, and that way Frank can stay off his leg."

"Great!" Frank said. "That's perfect."

"It's perfect, if you'll take me back to Prudhoe," Joe cut in. "There are a lot of ends to tie up there. There's the Hammond-White connection. And was that really Scott we saw? I mean, what would he be doing there? In some lab, after hours?"

"I'll take you," Virgil said. "Better go now. This way I can come back and then get a good start in the morning."

"Fine with me," Joe responded, getting up from the ground.

"Just don't get into trouble," Frank said. "We won't be around to help you out."

"What? Me? Get into trouble?" Joe smiled. "You've got to be kidding. I'm just going to do a little creative snooping, that's all."

"Right." Frank laughed. "Just don't get caught."

"You can always contact the weather pilot at the airport if you want to get in touch with us,"

Virgil volunteered. "He's a friend of mine, and he flies out over the ocean just about every day."

Joe nodded. "Fine. He's one of the first people I'll check in with."

"Who else do you know in Prudhoe?" Frank asked as Joe hurried to leave. "Wait a minute. Are you going to talk with Cindy?"

"That's for me to know, and you to find out." Joe grinned. "Catch you later."

He climbed into the helicopter. In a matter of minutes the chopper was a speck in the huge northern sky, and Frank was alone by the fire.

He stared into the flames, thinking. An image of buoys in some part of his mind kept insisting that this whole thing had something to do with the ocean.

Frank closed his eyes, trying to concentrate. But the fire and his rough day drugged him. Soon he was dozing. The flicker of the firelight played against his eyelids like a blinking light, like the safety buoys floating back home in Barmet Bay . . . .

Frank's eyes snapped open as he realized what was nagging him. He'd seen them *twice*. They'd found one on the plane, before they'd had to jump. Then there was the other one in the bunker at North Slope Supply.

He tried to call up an image of what they'd looked like. The one on the plane had a radio transponder. Well, that cinched it. That definitely explained *why* he kept thinking of the ocean. But

73

why would anyone want or need a floating radio set?

Frank's head jerked back as he pulled himself totally awake. A floating radio could pinpoint the high-seas rendezvous for an airplane—or a submarine.

Chapter

10

VIRGIL HAD HARDLY landed the chopper before Frank ran limping up to talk about his idea.

"You could be right," Virgil said. "Some of my friends think there's submarine activity up there."

"How would they know?" Frank asked.

"When things come out of a sub, they head up to the surface—oil, that kind of stuff," Virgil answered. "We'll see tomorrow."

They slept soundly and at midmorning set off in the helicopter for Virgil's fishing camp. The dogs were still there. Apparently someone came in to feed them every day while Virgil wasn't there. The boat was still sound and seaworthy, and soon they were chugging through the white-caps of the Arctic Ocean.

Virgil laughed as Tanook jumped aboard. "This dog loves fishing," he said.

The boat was sturdy, built more for endurance than speed. The engine was mounted on the back, and Virgil stored extra fuel and supplies under the seats. It was a craft made for the icy waters of the northern seas.

Frank sat in the center, Virgil at the stern, one hand on the tiller. Tanook took his station up front. He enjoyed the wind in his face, even though he did bark when hit by spray.

As they headed north Virgil tended to business, throwing out lines and catching fish. He threw them, alive, into the large wooden box in the middle of the boat. Some he would use for bait— others for food. One he threw to Tanook, who quickly gobbled it down.

"When autumn comes, all this will be dotted with pack ice," Virgil told Frank with a grin. "All the native people know. The best time to travel is in the wintertime."

Frank looked out over the black water. It was hard to imagine what it would look like a couple of months from then—white and frozen in the darkness of the Arctic winter.

After an hour of fishing Virgil pointed to a shiny spot on the water where the reflections from the sun were tinted with blue and red. "See that?" he called. "Oil. Not good for fish or seals!"

Frank had seen pictures of oil slicks in news

magazines, but this wasn't the same. "It doesn't look very big," he said.

"Big enough," Virgil muttered bitterly. "This had to come from a big ship—a freighter or a submarine."

They continued north, past the slick, then past still another one. Virgil scanned the horizon silently. Frank, too, fell into silence, prickling with the feeling that they were not alone. Something was out there with them. But all he heard was the droning of their engine as they plowed north.

Virgil turned off the engine without warning. The complete silence was a shock to Frank. He looked at Virgil to see if everything was all right. Virgil just held up a finger to his lips to silence him. His ear was cocked into the wind and he was gazing at nothing.

"I think I hear something," he said after a moment. "Listen."

Frank caught only the sounds of waves slapping against the side of the boat and of the wind.

"What do you think it is?" Frank whispered.

"A boat, or maybe a plane," Virgil said. He remained perfectly still. "I think it's coming up from the south."

Frank was amazed at Virgil's hearing. At the fishing camp, he'd heard the approaching choppers minutes before anyone else. Now he'd picked out the sound of a distant engine over all the wind and water.

But Frank was the first to catch the glint of sunlight on the plane's wings. "There it is!"

It showed only as a tiny speck against the white of the overcast clouds. But it became clearer as it drew nearer. "It's a seaplane," Frank said, "with pontoons."

"Not many planes come out here prepared to land on the water." Virgil cranked up the engine again, pointing the boat due north and opening the throttle. The bow rose out of the water as the propellers bit into the sea.

"How can we race a plane?" Frank asked.

"We're ahead of it already, and we can keep an eye on it for quite a while," Virgil said. "If we line up with its course, sooner or later we're bound to come across it when it lands."

They continued on in silence. Virgil no longer fished—he wrapped up all his lines and stowed them.

A thought occurred to Frank. "Do we have enough fuel?"

Virgil glanced down at the tanks. "Depends on how long we have to go. We can keep on for a couple more hours."

Frank sat back to enjoy the ride. What more could he want? His leg was feeling better; he had the smell of salt water and the wind—and maybe answers for a lot of questions.

The plane was long out of sight, but after two hours of following its course they caught up with it. There it was, bobbing on the water in the middle of nowhere.

Frank tapped Virgil's arm. "Better turn off the engine. We don't want them to think we're spying on them."

"What if we're fishing?" Virgil said with a grin. "That shouldn't be suspicious."

Throwing out some fishing lines, Virgil handed Frank a parka. "Pull the hood up," he suggested. "They may have binoculars."

Looking innocent and busy, Virgil started the engine, and they trolled slowly, moving constantly toward the seaplane. There was no sign of life either in or around it. Where was the pilot?

As they got closer Frank's eyes narrowed. "Hey, Virgil, that plane isn't moving around. I think it's anchored."

Virgil steered around it in a wide circle. After several minutes they were able to see the other side of the plane and they got a glimpse into the cockpit. Two men *were* inside, deep in conversation. They obviously hadn't seen the little fishing boat.

Bobbing up and down in the water, next to the plane, was a sea buoy with a radio transponder on it.

Frank grinned in triumph. "That could be the buoy they had on the plane we fell from, or one exactly like it. We may have tied these guys into the attempt to kidnap us. Now all we have to do is see what they're waiting for."

Virgil cut the engine and drifted. Because they were so low in the water, they were hidden by waves most of the time. They sat still with poles in their hands, but with both eyes on the plane.

Their work was soon rewarded, for the sea suddenly erupted yards from the plane. And a black hulking form lifted out of the waves like some sea behemoth. Frank and Virgil watched in stunned silence.

Shedding tons of seawater, the metal sea monster revealed itself to be the superstructure of a submarine. A hatch opened, and a man clambered along the sub's deck, holding a chain.

One of the men on the plane tossed a line to him, and he towed the plane up next to the sub.

A second man emerged from the hatch. Frank could see right away who it was. The sun picked out his blond hair, marking him as Sandy White.

"That's the guy who wired us to the polygraph," Frank whispered. "He's the president of North Slope Supply."

"Are you sure?" Virgil asked.

"Positive," Frank said. White was giving orders to the man who'd fastened the ropes. Then he stopped, his eyes scanning the horizon. Frank had the uncomfortable feeling that White had spotted them.

White moved to the plane and reached out. The pilot tossed him something. For a second White held his hands up to his eyes. Then he turned to the sailor, who quickly turned and disappeared down the hatch.

White's hands went back to his eyes. This time, sunlight reflected off the polished lenses. "Binoculars!" Frank said. "He has spotted us!"

A crew of four came tumbling out of the hatch, dragging something. Frank recognized it as an inflatable boat and an outboard motor.

"We'd better get out of here," he said. "If they catch us, White will recognize me."

"Okay, here we go," Virgil said.

He gunned the motor, turning the boat south as they heard another engine ripping into life behind them. "That sucker inflates fast," Virgil said.

Frank looked around, his mouth set in a straight line. "It moves fast, too."

The inflatable craft was tiny but high-powered. And it was gaining on them with every second.

Chapter

11

WHEN JOE ARRIVED in Prudhoe, the first thing he did was change hotels once again and get some sleep. Then later that day he set himself up on a stakeout.

When quitting time came for Trans-Yukon, Joe was reading a newspaper, sitting on a low wall across the street from their offices. He kept his face covered while keeping an eye on the workers. Finally Cindy Velikov opened the heavy glass door and stepped out into the late-afternoon sunshine. She buttoned her coat as she strolled across town on foot.

Joe followed her, but it wasn't easy to keep his distance. Her steps were small compared to Joe's normal impatient stride. He had to force himself to maintain a leisurely gait and stop frequently, as though he were basking in the warm weather.

She went into a grocery store, but Joe didn't dare to go inside. When Cindy came out she had a small brown bag of groceries in her arms. She continued to walk, now into a residential area.

After a few more turns she walked up to the back door of a small red ranch house. Joe walked past. He went to the end of the block, checking to make sure he wasn't being tailed. Then he walked around to the back door and knocked.

She stood behind the screen, staring out at him. For a minute she didn't know Joe. Then, after she recognized him, she smiled broadly and opened the door.

"Joe Hardy!" She grinned.

Joe smiled back. "That's me," he said. "I hope you don't mind. I followed you home because I want to talk to you."

"No, I don't mind," she said. "Come in."

Cindy opened the door, and Joe stepped into the kitchen. The floor was terra-cotta tiles, and the appliances were all new. White café curtains covered half the window above the sink.

Cindy laughed. "What are you staring at?"

"Sorry," Joe said. "I guess I was a little surprised—your kitchen looks so modern."

"I guess you were expecting a log cabin with a water pump in the kitchen and an outhouse." Her eyes twinkled as she spoke. "We are part of the United States, you know—just bigger and better." She made a sweeping gesture with her hands, reminding Joe of what he'd said about New York City. They laughed.

"So, what would you like to talk to me about?" she asked.

Joe came straight out with it. "I want to find out about what's going on with your company."

Cindy nodded. "Okay," she said. "But I think we'd better take a walk. My father will be home soon, and I don't want him to hear this."

She picked up her coat, and they left through the kitchen door.

"Oops," Cindy said, turning around. "I'd better leave my dad a note, so he doesn't worry." She ducked into the kitchen again and was back a moment later.

They headed out to the street, both with their hands in their pockets. Joe spoke first.

"I never thanked you for warning us that night," he said. "Did you hear anything from your side about what happened to us?"

Cindy shrugged. "No. I thought you'd left the state."

"We almost did—the hard way. A bunch of guys jumped us and threw us on a plane. We barely escaped."

"You should have left when I warned you." Cindy turned to Joe. "My boss isn't a very nice man."

"So why do you work for him?"

"Jobs aren't so easy to get up here. I've had this one for a few years, and I'm saving money to go to college." She shrugged. "And Mr. Hammond wasn't always this way."

"What way? He seems friendly."

"Sure, he's friendly. But I think he's involved in something crooked. He's been hiring weird people we don't need, and firing men who've worked for him for years. The place has really changed over the last six months."

"How do you know all this?" Joe asked.

"I update the personnel records, so I see everything that's going on. Mr. Hammond thinks I don't pay any attention, but I do. We were letting people go because of money problems, then all this weird hiring began.

"But I can't prove that anything wrong is going on," Cindy continued. "And also, no one who's suspicious wants to be labeled as a trouble maker. This is a small town," she said, glancing around at the little houses that lined the streets. "And we have just a few big companies. Mr. Hammond is a powerful person here. He knows all the other bosses. If the men who got fired grumble too loudly, they won't get any work."

Joe saw what he was up against. "You said it wasn't always like this—so who changed things? Who's spreading the bribes around?"

"I have no idea." Cindy shook her head. "At first I thought it was just a trickle of guys from the lower forty-eight states, up here looking for work. In hard times, they'll pay for their first job."

"Does that make sense?" Joe asked, trying to imagine how anyone could afford to do such a thing.

"For some of them, it does. When jobs are scarce up here, people are willing to do just about anything. See, the pay is very high. If you're willing to live cheaply here, you can save quite a bit."

"You mean a guy could come up here, bribe someone to get a job, make a living, and still save money?"

"Exactly. They do it all the time. It's not a comfortable life, but they can make a bundle, even with the bribes they have to pay."

"You said 'at first.' Do you think it's just a guy here and there paying Hammond for jobs?"

Cindy shook her head, her blond hair brushing her shoulders. "It's been happening too regularly. And the people all wind up getting the same job."

"What job?" Joe asked.

"I don't know exactly what they call it. Trans-Yukon has a contract to maintain parts of the pipeline. They cut brush, scrape ice off—even clean the inside of the pipes. It seems like that's the job that the bribes were about—the inside job."

"You mean people actually go into the pipe to clean it?"

Cindy nodded. "It'a a really dirty job, but it's

got to be done—to make sure everything's okay."

Pieces began coming together for Joe. "Millions of dollars of oil flow through the pipeline. Suppose somebody could go up in the mountains where no one is around and sabotage the whole operation?"

"There's a security system," Cindy said. "The pipe has to be guarded."

"Well, if I was going to pay Hammond for a job, I'd want to be a guard on the outside, rather than do the dirty work inside."

"There's one other thing. I heard about some kind of a deal between Hammond and White going down on Sawtooth Mountain tomorrow morning."

"Guess who'll be there to greet them," Joe said, curious.

They'd arrived in the business district of Prudhoe, just a few blocks from the waterfront.

"Would you like to walk over to the water?" Cindy asked.

"Fine," Joe said. He was still trying to figure how North Slope and Scott Sanders fit into the story.

The docks weren't pretty. They were a jumble of serious industrial equipment spread along a cold, flat, unfriendly coastline. Still, there was something exciting about walking past the huge tankers, pipes, and pumps. It gave the feeling of important business being conducted, even at the edge of the world.

Joe and Cindy stopped on the street that looked out over the busy port. The sound of engines and the heavy clang of hammers beat through the air. It was just past seven o'clock in the evening, but the sun was high and the light was reddish gold.

"I've lived here all my life," Cindy said. "My father is a descendant of the original Russian settlers. My mother was the daughter of an air force captain stationed here. She died a couple of years ago."

"I'm sorry to hear that," Joe said.

"This is all I know. I'd really like to get out of here. You know, see the world. I feel as if I know next to nothing."

"Well, there's plenty to see," Joe said. "It seems to me you know a lot about things around here."

"Maybe too much," a rasping voice hissed from behind them. When they pivoted around, they were smack up against a huge, towering guy.

"Maybe Mr. Hammond should hear just how much you know about things around here." The man had a thick wool cap pulled down over a square, fleshy face. When he took his hands out of his pockets, Joe stared. These were the biggest hands Joe had ever seen, thick and broad, with bulging knuckles and callused skin. If this guy made a fist, it would nearly be the size of Joe's head.

"Come on, you two," the man growled. "We've got a date with Mr. Hammond."

One huge paw shoved at Joe's shoulder, forcing him to walk in front.

Joe's fists clenched. How could he not have known they were being tailed? He was furious.

"Don't try anything, pal," the thug warned. "I'm holding on to the girl's arm right now. But I could just as easily grab her neck." He laughed. "You wouldn't want that, would you?"

Chapter

12

"PLEASE, JOE, DO what he says." Cindy sounded terrified. When Joe glanced back, he saw the tears that lined her eyes.

"Keep walking," growled the man. "Never mind what's going on back here." Joe forced himself to step out. He could hear Hammond's goon wheezing as he lumbered along behind.

Joe's mind flicked frantically from one plan to another. He had to nail this guy. But how? He was stuck out front, and the guy had Cindy for a hostage. Anything Joe might do to let Cindy get away would get him creamed. But he couldn't just run for it and leave Cindy. Nor would he be delivered to Spike Hammond, all wrapped up like a Christmas present.

Somehow, he had to get the edge on this guy. He'd have to watch and hope for an opportunity.

The streets they were on now, down by the docks, were narrow and gray. Low buildings, mostly warehouses, squatted under the arctic sky. Many of the roads were dirt—grass, moss, and lichen grew wherever cars and feet hadn't trampled them.

"Turn here," Hammond's goon commanded.

Joe followed his directions. They were walking away from the waterfront and toward the center of town. It was quiet and deserted, but not too far off they could hear the sound of music and men's laughter. Maybe there was a chance after all.

To set things up, Joe decided on a little distraction. "So tell me," he said over his shoulder as he continued to walk, "does Hammond give you a piece of his action?"

"None of your business."

"Hammond's raking it in with his bribe scam," Joe went on. "I hope you're getting some."

"I do all right. I'm on retainer," the goon said in a proud voice.

"Like a lawyer," Joe said. "But I bet he doesn't pay your medical expenses."

"Why should he?"

"Because someday someone will knock your stupid head off, and the doctors are going to have to sew it back on."

Joe had timed the zinger perfectly. They'd just reached an area with fast-food joints, stores, video-game parlors, and a movie theater. Man-mountain couldn't do anything to him here.

He could hear the thug's teeth grinding together. "Just keep your mouth shut, punk. I'll take care of you later."

They were passing a video-game parlor as a crowd of men came spilling out onto the sidewalk. They were laughing and cheering as two of them broke into a sparring match. The fighters held their fists high and danced in circles around each other, ducking and weaving, flicking hard knuckles toward grinning faces. It was all in fun—none of the jabs were connecting. But the crowd made a big thing out of each near-miss.

One of the fighters lost his balance and bumped into Joe. A chance! Joe spun the off-balance boxer back into Cindy and the goon. The guy found himself with his arms around Cindy, and before he could get loose, Joe jumped in.

"Keep your hands off my friend's girl," he yelled, taking a huge wind-up with his right hand. The punch was more like a slap. Everyone in the street heard the *crack* of Joe's hand on the boxer's cheek.

The crowd became quiet—too quiet. They were mad. It was one thing to have a friendly sparring match with a buddy. It was another to see some stranger haul off and slug that buddy in the face.

"Get him!" somebody yelled, heading toward Joe. "Fix that punk's face for him!"

Joe stood his ground in front of Cindy as the

crowd surged forward. He took some punches but also threw a few good ones, to keep these guys good and angry. Retreating a bit, he risked a look back toward Cindy. Hammond's goon still held her arm in a tight grip.

Jumping behind the confused thug, Joe yelled, "Come on, pal, I'm not fighting them all for you. She's your girl, after all."

Figuring the goon was with Joe, the crowd began to jostle him. Man-mountain shoved them away, but they shoved back and then began throwing punches. It was perfect. He lost his temper, dropped Cindy's arm, and waded into the crowd, slugging at everybody.

While the thug was busy getting mobbed, Joe grabbed Cindy by the wrist and pulled her down the street. "Come on! Now's our chance!"

As they ran the yelling and groaning faded behind them. Joe glanced back as they rounded a corner and saw that the goon had belatedly realized what was going on. He was pulling out of the fight.

Joe and Cindy ducked around another corner and found themselves in a narrow back street, barely wide enough for a single car. Joe led the way, running as fast as he could while towing Cindy. He tried the first door they came to, hoping to duck before Hammond's thug could see where they'd gone. The door was open, so they stepped inside, yanking it shut behind them.

Their hiding place was dark, with flickering

light glistening in the air behind them. Joe stared around in confusion until it hit him. They were standing behind a movie screen. The flickering light came from the film being projected onto the thin silvery sheet in front of them. They were standing in the back of the movie theater, looking at the reverse images of the film.

"We'd better get away from the door," Joe whispered. "Follow me."

They tiptoed along the back wall to a dark corner on the far side of the stage. As soon as they reached it the outside door banged open, and the thug peered in.

Joe looked around for an escape route. An iron ladder, mounted on the cinder-block wall, was just to his left. He silently motioned for Cindy to climb up. As soon as she reached the catwalk at the top, Joe followed.

Once they were on the dark catwalk, he whispered in her ear, "We had to make our move before his eyes adjusted to the dark."

They both stared down as their pursuer searched the backstage area. The images from the film swam across his clothes. Music blared loudly from speakers placed directly behind the screen. The thug reached the dark corner where they'd stood a minute before. And Cindy gasped out loud. Too loud. The guy glanced up.

Joe climbed over the railing and dropped on top of the man standing below. He made a perfect landing, knocking the guy flat to the floor. Immediately they began to grapple. But thanks to his huge bulk the thug quickly got the upper hand, pinning Joe to the floor.

With a quick jerk Joe managed to get his hands free, and he clapped them together hard over the thug's ears. The pain threw the guy off balance, and Joe took advantage of that to shove him back onto the floor again.

Leaping to his feet, Joe jumped on him. But the thug was a born street fighter. He rolled aside and lunged toward the wall, where a large flashlight hung from a hook. Grabbing it, he swung it viciously at Joe's head, catching him on the ear.

Joe staggered, his ear ringing, his vision going red. He was two seconds from being out cold— but he was also madder than he'd felt in a long time. Ignoring the pain, he waited for the guy to swing again, and when it happened, he ducked. The flashlight passed over his head, leaving the goon wide open.

Putting all his weight behind a solid uppercut, Joe caught the guy right on the chin. He toppled slowly to his knees, the fight knocked out of him.

Joe yanked the flashlight from the man's hand, pushed him to the floor, and sat on his chest. "Now talk," he whispered angrily. "What's Hammond up to?"

"I don't know," he groaned.

"You'd better stop stalling," Joe warned, his voice covered by the soundtrack from the film.

"Unless you want to be swept up by the ushers after the midnight show."

"All right. We're getting a big payment up on Sawtooth Mountain in the morning. That's all I know. The boss wants everything to go smoothly," the goon mumbled.

"Who's giving you the money?"

"I swear I don't know. Different people every time."

"You'd better be telling the truth," Joe growled. "Now get over there by the ladder."

The man crawled across the floor and leaned against the wall. Joe motioned for Cindy to come down. They undid the goon's belt to use to tie him to the iron bars of the ladder and shoved a handkerchief into his mouth.

Turning on the flashlight, Joe escorted Cindy around the edge of the screen, down the steps, and up the main aisle of the theater.

"We look official, don't we?" he joked. "Just like an usher and a customer."

There was no one in the lobby out front. They left the light on the ledge outside the box office and stepped out into the bright night.

"I've got to get in touch with Frank. Do you know anyone with a ham radio?" he asked.

"Yes—my father," Cindy said excitedly. "He keeps it in the basement."

He grinned. "Great. Let's go!" Once again they were running through the streets.

Cindy's father wasn't home, but Joe was able

to get the set going. He put out a call every five minutes for over two hours, but there was no response.

"This isn't good. I know Virgil keeps his radio on." He tried a few more times, but he was getting anxious. "We've got to get ahold of them."

Cindy left him twiddling dials on the radio set. "I'll make some supper." But she'd hardly reached the kitchen when Joe came bounding up the stairs.

"We've got to go to the airport. I just talked to the guy who flies the weather plane. He's a friend of Virgil's, and he'll take us out over the ocean to find them."

Cindy turned off the stove and got the keys to her dad's car. She drove like a pro to the airport, where they found the pilot sipping coffee in front of the hanger.

In less than ten minutes they were in the air, scouting the gray waters of the Arctic Ocean. Joe's eyes were getting tired when he saw something floating in the water.

"What's that?" he asked, pointing.

The pilot glanced over. "First iceberg of the season." He dipped the plane for a closer look.

But floating behind the ice was a boat. Joe trained his binoculars on it. Yes, he recognized that boat—it was Virgil's.

And it was empty, drifting aimlessly on the cold vastness of the silent sea.

Chapter

13

SEVERAL HOURS EARLIER Frank and Virgil had been speeding through the rough waters, trying to outrun the inflatable speedboat.

"There's no way we're going to outrun these guys," Virgil shouted over the noise of the churning engine. Ice-cold water sprayed up from the bow of Virgil's little fishing craft as it bounced over the waves. Tanook, who'd been lying peacefully on the floor of the boat, was up now, his nose pointing anxiously into the wind, his ears flattened against his head.

Frank looked back. Their pursuers seemed to be flying over the water.

"That must be some kind of a high-tech machine," Frank shouted. "If we can't outrun it, what do we do?"

"We need to find some pack ice," Virgil yelled.

"It might give us an advantage." He scanned the horizon for icebergs.

They plowed through the choppy seas. Frank clung to his seat, not only to keep his balance but also to keep his leg as straight as possible. He didn't want to tear open his wound by falling when the boat hit the trough of a wave. Virgil, meanwhile, had stood up in the stern, one hand on the tiller. His dark eyes squinted into the gray distance.

He sat abruptly, steering the boat on a new course. "Ice," he said briefly. They quickly reached a cluster of icebergs, and he nosed the boat in, looking for a crack between the huge chunks. Finding one, he drove the boat into the narrow passage. The sides of the boat scraped along the ice, but by keeping the engine going, Virgil was able to nudge some of the smaller ice fragments away.

"We might be able to hide in here," he said, running the engine slower. "They'll be afraid to come in."

The pack ice glistened around them, white and blue. Some pieces were tall, towering over the boat, giving them protection not only from the wind but from their pursuers. Other pieces were flat, riding in the water like traveling islands. Virgil drove the boat skillfully through the little channels between the chunks.

Once they reached the shelter of several big bergs, Virgil cut the engine altogether, and they drifted. They could hear the engine of the other boat bearing down on them.

"I think we'd better give them one more look at us," Virgil said.

"What for?" Frank asked. "Aren't we safer in here?"

"Uh-uh," Virgil said. "They've got to think we're dead. So we'll pretend to capsize."

"How're you going to . . .?"

Virgil gunned the boat back out into the open water. The attackers were within firing range, bouncing along on a high crest. Two shots rang out, then Virgil banked into a steep turn and circled the first part of the ice pack. Suddenly they were on the other side of a tall berg.

"The last thing they saw was our turn," Virgil said. "That's very dangerous in this water. Now—we have to move fast." He cut off the engine. "Unravel that fishing line. We've got to set up a trick."

They drifted up against the edge of the ice. Virgil leapt out and drove a metal spike deep into the granular snow that covered the surface of the berg. Then, taking the transparent fishing line, he tied one end to the stake and the other to a hook protruding from his boat at the water line. He made sure the stake was set securely, then covered it with snow. Then he took a weight and tied it to the line.

"Good. That'll make it sink," he said. "Okay, everybody out." Frank and Tanook jumped onto the iceberg. Frank was hobbling. Tanook was wagging his tail and looking from Virgil to Frank.

"I hope this works," Virgil said. "I'm going to make it look like we tipped over." With an empty plastic container, he shoveled water into the boat. When a substantial puddle had collected on the bottom, he shoved the boat away and toward the open passage to the sea. The wind and the waves pushed it the rest of the way into open water. The fishing line was completely invisible.

"Okay, let's hide," he said. "This way." They hurried across the relatively flat surface of the iceberg, their feet crunching the snow.

"Tanook first," Virgil said. He picked out a place where Tanook could hide. After making the dog lie down, he began covering him with snow. In a few minutes, Tanook had completely disappeared.

"Stay!" Virgil commanded. Tanook did not move. "Good boy!"

Virgil walked away, feeling for the depth of the snow with his feet. When he found a place that he liked, he motioned for Frank to lie down.

"You hide here. The snow will protect you."

Frank lay down, warm in the heavy parka Virgil had given him. With large chunks, then handfuls of finer powder, Virgil proceeded to bury Frank, leaving him airholes.

"Okay?" Virgil called.

"Fine!" Frank replied, making sure his leg was in a comfortable position.

"Just in time. Here they come."

Frank heard Virgil burrowing into the snow next to him. Then the *brrr* of the pursuit boat's engine reached his ears. It sounded as if they were circling Virgil's abandoned boat. Frank hoped they wouldn't find the transparent lifeline, or worse, run afoul of it. If their propeller cut it, Virgil's boat would be adrift for real.

The engine drone moved back and forth in front of the ice pack. They must be looking for our bodies, Frank thought. Then he heard nothing. The engine had been cut off—it hadn't died away. Moments later the sound of human voices broke the silence.

Then came the crunch of footsteps on the snow. What if they see our footprints? Frank suddenly thought.

Judging from the direction of the voices, the men from the sub had landed quite a distance from where Frank and his friends were hidden.

"We check it out," one voice said in a thick accent. "Is better to be sure."

Frank heard rattles and scrapes—someone was climbing the little hill in the center of the ice island. A new voice asked something in a foreign language.

"Remember orders—we talk English," the first voice growled. "I see nothing here. We go back to sub—get ready for the drop at Sawtooth."

Next came a skidding sound, then the crunching and squeaking of feet on snow.

"Probably drowned, those kids," the second voice said.

So, White recognized me, and figures Virgil must be Joe, Frank thought. Good. We have another surprise to hit them with. He lay as still as possible as the voices drew nearer.

Suddenly they were very close.

"Footprints?" one man said.

They stopped to examine the tracks. "Could be seals—or polar bears."

"Seals, I think. No polar bears here. Or kids, either, I think—not unless they throw their boat away."

The searchers laughed. "We go back, tell about drowned boys."

Frank heard them walk away with relief. But wait a second—they were heading toward Tanook.

How could a dog—even as intelligent a dog as Tanook—remain under the snow? Frank was thinking to himself. "Please, Tanook, be good," Frank muttered under his breath. "Please!"

From the sound of things, Tanook did remain still—right until one of the searchers stepped on him. Frank heard a yelp and a growl, a wild yell from one of the men, and then a gunshot.

Frank pushed his way up to peek from his hiding place. Tanook must have gone for one searcher's wrist—since he could see a revolver on the snow. The man was howling, nearly drowning out Tanook's growls.

The other crewman kept circling the struggling pair, trying to get a good shot at Tanook. The dog was twisting and jumping so much that it was hard to take aim. Frank saw the man raise his gun, then lower it, afraid of shooting his comrade.

Then Tanook switched his grip and lunged for the man's throat. The man reeled back, throwing his hands up to protect himself. Tanook smashed into his chest. The other man took steady aim at the dog, and then Frank leapt up from his snow grave with a shout.

The man with the gun whirled toward Frank and snapped off a wild shot. At the same time his buddy pushed Tanook away—and tottered off the iceberg.

He hit the freezing black water and had time for one desperate cry before he went into shock. Perhaps it was merciful. The man's white face was stiffening even as he sank below the surface.

Everything had halted for that horrible moment. Even Tanook stood still, staring at the water as if he couldn't believe what had happened.

The remaining seaman looked shocked, but he was well trained, and he knew his business. His gun hand was rock steady, the revolver aimed dead on target—right at Frank's heart.

Chapter

14

VIRGIL SPRANG FROM his hiding place like a missile launched from an underground silo. Now the gunman had to turn and face yet another enemy. He didn't know which way to point his gun.

Tanook crouched and growled, his teeth bared. Frank turned sideways so he'd be a smaller target. Virgil began to speak to Tanook in his native language.

The man with the gun spoke. "You come with me," he said nervously, pointing the gun first at Frank, then at Virgil, all the while keeping an eye on Tanook, who was creeping closer.

"Come and get us," Frank said boldly.

The man glared, then fired at Frank—and missed. His revolver was a snub-nose, and Frank was a good thirty yards away. Virgil hit the ground at the sound of the gun. That was wise, since the gunman whirled, squeezing off a shot in his direction. The bullet whizzed inches above Virgil's prone body. The gunman turned on Tanook. Too late.

Tanook was leaping as the gunman snapped off another shot. Tanook twisted in midair and came in at waist level, his teeth sinking into the wrist of the guy's gun hand.

With Tanook holding the gun down, Frank had a chance. He bent his good knee and hurled himself across the snow to join in the struggle. The man was still clutching his pistol, fighting to grab the gun with his free hand. That's when Frank landed, flattening the guy.

"Nice work, Tanook," Frank said, patting the dog. The man's body was limp, and Tanook let go of the wrist. Frank took the gun.

"Only one bullet left," he said, glancing in the chamber. Then he looked down at the man who lay unconscious in the snow. "Sorry to gang up on you, pal, but we had no choice."

"Who is he?" Virgil asked, staring at the man's pale face.

"He works for Sandy White, that's all I know. When he was talking with his buddy, they mentioned something about Sawtooth. Does that mean anything to you?" Frank asked as he knelt down to check the man's vital signs.

"Yes. There's a mountain called Sawtooth."

"I think that'll be our next stop," Frank said. "We've got to figure out, once and for all, what

White and Hammond are up to. Let's get your boat and head out of here.''

Virgil shook his head. "We'd waste time—better take their boat." He looked around worriedly. "Maybe the ice walls kept in the sounds of the gunshots. If not—well, sound travels pretty far over open water. I'd like to be out of here. We can leave my boat for Sleeping Beauty here."

After checking the amount of fuel left in the inflatable speed boat, they started the engine and headed for Virgil's fishing camp. It was a fast but uncomfortable trip.

Joe's face was grim as he sat deep in thought aboard the weather plane. What had happened to Frank and Virgil? The abandoned boat, floating in the middle of the ocean, was a haunting sight. He hardly dared think about it.

"You've got to take us to Sawtooth Mountain. Can you do that?" he asked the pilot.

"Sure can. But there's no way I can land. You'll have to jump. I've got some chutes in the back."

"I don't think Cindy should jump," Joe said, looking at the girl beside him. "Maybe you should go back to Prudhoe."

"No way!" Cindy shouted. "I'm not going there. They know where I live, and chances are that fat guy got away and told Hammond I was with you."

107

"But you could hang out at a friend's house until this thing gets settled," Joe suggested.

Cindy fixed her eyes on Joe. "Read my lips," she said. "The answer is *N-O*. I'm going with you!"

"Okay, if that's what you want," Joe said, throwing up his hands. "It's not going to be much fun. Your boss likes to play hardball."

"Ex-boss," Cindy told him.

They climbed into the back of the plane and strapped on parachutes. Joe had to show Cindy how to do it and teach her how to pull her cord.

"I'll be right with you," he said. "It's easy. Don't be afraid. And when you land, keep your knees slightly bent."

Cindy nodded and bit her lip. It was clear she was scared but determined to go through with the jump anyway.

"We'll be there in a few minutes," the pilot said.

"What time is it?" Joe asked.

"About two in the morning. You'll have to wait for a while once you get there."

"That's okay. We'll find a hiding place where we can keep an eye on things. If you don't hear from us in a day or two, would you come looking? And tell Virgil, if you see him."

"Will do," the pilot said. "We're coming up on Sawtooth now. Get ready to jump."

Joe slid the side door of the plane open, and a

fierce rush of cold air hit him like a wall. Taking Cindy's hand, he walked her to the edge of the door. He gave her a reassuring smile, then held her hand as they dived out of the plane.

They fell through the pale sky for only a few seconds before pulling their rip cords. Joe had no idea where they'd land, but he figured it would look like much of the Brooks Range—rocky, treeless tundra covered with arctic moss and wild blueberries. The only danger could be the occasional stand of white spruce, which could reach a height of twenty feet. But the trees usually only grew in sheltered valleys, and they were supposed to land near the summit of Sawtooth Mountain.

Joe could see the ground coming up fast now. It was hard to tell what it looked like. With only half light, the terrain looked flat. But Joe knew that was an illusion. As he got closer he saw they'd be landing right on the side of the mountain.

He hit first, drifting up into the slope of the hill. He kept his balance and landed perfectly.

Instantly he looked up for Cindy. There she was, drifting out of the sky under the webbing of her chute. She looked a little like a fly struggling in a spider's web. She moved her legs in anticipation of the landing and held on to the lines for dear life.

When she hit the slope of the mountain, Cindy hit hard. But Joe had disengaged himself from his own chute and was running to help her. She would be bruised, but basically unhurt.

"Gather up your chute and follow me," he said. "We're going to climb."

They collected the billowing folds of their parachutes like huge armfuls of laundry. Then, tucking them under their arms, they clambered up the steep, rocky slope of Sawtooth Mountain.

At the peak they found a safe hiding place—a rocky ledge, out of the wind and, even more important, hard to see from the air. They would be mostly covered by a huge boulder that perched on the side of the slope.

"This is perfect," Joe said. "We can get some sleep here, and we won't have to worry about being seen." He began to spread out his parachute.

"You mean you're going to try to sleep here?" Cindy asked in disbelief. "It's so rocky!"

"It's perfect. Protected, cozy—we've even got blankets."

Joe lay down on his parachute and then rolled himself up in it. Cindy reluctantly did the same. They were so tired that despite the rocks and the roar of the wind they were both sound asleep in a few minutes.

They were awakened in the morning by the *whirr* of an approaching helicopter. Crouching close to their rock, Joe and Cindy watched as the chopper landed on the desolate mountaintop a few yards away from them. Four men got out, including Spike Hammond. They stood around their silent copter, staring off into the sky.

A few minutes passed. Another chopper came rattling in from the north and landed even closer to Joe. He crept around the boulder to get a look inside the pilot's bubble. The pilot was alone—but Joe did see a MAC-10 submachine gun leaning up against the copilot's seat.

As Joe watched, the pilot grabbed a large leather bag off the floor and hopped out, leaving the engine on and the door open. Joe didn't recognize him. He walked over to Spike Hammond and shook hands. Joe tried to hear what they were saying, but the roar of the engine and the thrumming blades made it impossible.

Hammond and the pilot talked for a minute or so, then the pilot handed Hammond the bag. Apparently Hammond wanted to check it out. He set the bag down, undoing a buckle that held it closed. Joe took a chance. Leaning farther around the boulder, he tried to get a look inside the bag. When Hammond tipped it over, Joe got a glimpse. It was filled with money.

He decided to act.

"Stay down. If anything happens, hide out until the weather pilot sends someone to look for us," he whispered to Cindy.

"What are you going to do?" she asked, staring at him, eyes like saucers.

"I've got to stop them. I can't hear what

they're planning, but it can't be anything good. I've got to do something.''

Cindy grabbed his arm. "But, Joe, there's no one to help you!"

"I can't wait." Joe's face was grim as he pulled away.

Carrying his parachute slung over his shoulder, he ducked around the rock and sprinted for the nearest chopper. As he neared it he threw the chute up into the slowly rotating blades. The nylon caught in the rotors, fouling the engine. It sputtered to a halt, and Joe grabbed the MAC-10 inside. Then, coming around the fuselage of the chopper, he took command of the startled group.

"On the ground, all of you!" Joe shouted, pointing the submachine gun at them. The five conspirators froze in shock.

"Now!" Joe squeezed the trigger, sending a hail of bullets into the air just above their heads. They dove for the ground like soldiers in a drill.

Cautiously, Joe stepped out from behind the helicopter. He kept the gun level as he moved to recover the bag. Just as he was reaching for it he caught a flicker of movement from the corner of his eye.

Great, Joe thought. He could see a figure at the far end of the summit—a human silhouette moving against the gray of the sky.

Joe kept moving as if he hadn't noticed a thing,

his eyes flashing from his prisoners to the bag to the oncoming figure.

His hand tightened on the grip of the MAC-10. He calculated he had about two seconds to whirl, nail the ambushers, then return to cover the men on the ground.

Chapter

15

"DON'T SHOOT!" A familiar voice cried out as Joe whipped around. But Joe was already triggering the submachine gun.

At the last moment he jerked up the short barrel, and the figure flattened itself against the ground. The deadly spray of bullets flew into the blank silver sky.

"Hold your fire, Joe! It's me, Frank!" Joe would have a hard time identifying his brother. Frank lay flat with his cheek against the moss. But his voice was unmistakable.

"Frank, you maniac. I could've killed you!" Joe said, half-scolding, half-delighted. But this wasn't the time for a chat. As soon as his attention had been distracted from the prisoners they had started for their revolvers.

"Hold it right there!" Joe ripped off another

114

round of automatic fire, tearing up some of the tufts of moss between the prone figures.

"Don't anyone move a muscle," he ordered.

Frank stood up and approached Joe with the revolver he'd taken from the man on the iceberg. Virgil came over the lip of the mountain with Tanook at his side. When he saw the number of men on the ground, he looked amazed.

"How'd you get here?" Frank asked.

"It's a long story. Hammond had a tail on Cindy. Some thug of his tried to bring us in—I got him to talk. What happened to you? I saw your boat bobbing out on the ocean."

"That's the least of it," Frank said. "We saw lots of interesting stuff, including Sandy White on a submarine. I think you might call North Slope an offshore company."

"I guess so, if the head office is in a submarine," Joe joked. "But it begins to explain why he was so interested when we mentioned the Network. That might make a foreign agent nervous."

Frank nodded. "Especially if the foreign agent was spreading bribe money around and kidnapping people. But we still don't know what he's up to or how Scott fits in. Maybe we can find out from the guy who brought the payoffs."

Joe pointed to the skinny, dark pilot with the stubbly beard who'd stepped out of the chopper. "He's the one. I fouled his rotor with my parachute and, uh, borrowed this gun from his copter. That bag over there is full of money.''

"Keep me covered," Frank said. "I'm going to ask a few questions." He took a step, limping slightly, but suddenly spun around. Something had moved behind a boulder on the edge of the summit. He dropped into a crouch, aiming his revolver.

"Don't, Frank. It's Cindy. I forgot to tell you she was with me."

Cindy came out from behind the boulder, looking nervously at Frank.

"Joe, you should have told me. I almost shot her! Sorry, Cindy," he said, apologizing. She smiled weakly. "Maybe you can help us fill in some details."

"I'll do my best," Cindy said, looking at Spike Hammond, whose face had gone beet red.

But Frank ignored the construction boss, concentrating on the man who'd brought the money. Leaning over the guy, he asked, "Are you ready to talk?"

The man continued to lie facedown on the ground. "I have nothing to say."

"We'll see about that," Frank said. "What are you doing here?"

"What does it look like? I'm giving this man some money."

"What for?" Frank asked.

"It's my job," the man snarled into the dirt. "I fly a chopper and make deliveries."

"Where's Scott Sanders?"

"Who's that?"

"We saw him in the office building at North Slope headquarters."

"If you saw him, why ask me where he is?"

Frank was getting nowhere. This guy wouldn't give away anything. In fact, he didn't even look at Frank. He kept his gaze flat on the ground.

Time to change tactics, Frank decided. "What about you, Mr. Hammond?" he asked, turning to the large, redheaded man. "Guess you can't keep pretending you don't know what's going on, can you?"

"I'd like to know what *you* think you're doing," Hammond blustered, "bursting in on an innocent business meeting, hijacking—"

"Innocent?" Frank cut in. "Do you usually hold meetings on mountaintops—with people delivering bags of money?" He looked around the bare slope. "Or maybe this is the Bank of Sawtooth, and this fellow is the head teller."

Hammond said nothing. He was obviously feeling very uncomfortable.

"Do you know who this guy is?" Frank prodded Hammond, pointing at the skinny bag man.

"No, I don't," Hammond snapped back.

"If you want to keep lying on this cold ground, that's fine with me," Frank said. "But you might try being a little more helpful. So you don't know this guy personally. How about the people he's working for? I'd guess you'd check out an organization before doing business with it—even if it's dirty business. Who are they, and what are they up to?"

Hammond shifted his gaze warily. "I—uh, we tried, and got no—" Then his face hardened. "I don't see why I should tell you anything, just because you come along with a cock-and-bull story about a submarine."

"A submarine that I saw Sandy White, the president of North Slope Supply, climb out of. He saw us, too, and sent a couple of thugs after me and my friend here," Frank said.

"Well, that doesn't mean anything!" Hammond's voice was loud, but his tone was worried.

"Come on, Hammond. White isn't using that sub to set up underwater oil wells. He's using it as a base. And if he can afford a submarine, it means there's a pretty big organization behind him—like a government. How many unfriendly governments are close to Alaska?"

The big businessman's face went pale as this sank in.

"So, we've got a foreign agent handing around lots of money. What does he get in return?"

"North Slope asked if we could put some of their guys on our payroll, that's all. We were hurting, and they gave us a cheap loan—in several installments. What's the harm in that?"

"No harm, except to the guys you had to fire—

and to the morale of the rest of your workers, who hoped for promotions," Frank said.

"It happens all the time," Hammond said. "You have a friend whose nephew needs a job, so you help out—knowing he'll help you out on a deal down the line. That's the way it works."

"I guess White must have quite a few nephews," Frank shot back. "You're accepting money for these guys, and you don't even know who they are!"

"I don't need to know," Hammond replied. "They aren't hurting anybody."

"Oh, no? They attacked and threatened a friend of ours, kidnapped another, and tried to kill us. Remember how you called White to tell him about us?"

Hammond glared at Cindy when he heard this.

Frank stepped in front of him. "Your pals from North Slope grabbed us and stowed us aboard a plane heading into the Arctic Ocean. It was going to drop the signal buoy for the sub's rendezvous." He stared hard at Hammond. "And you know what? They were going to drop us right along with it."

"I—I didn't know," Hammond said, still more shaken.

"He can't prove a thing," the bagman suddenly spoke up. "Who would listen to this wild story about submarines and spies?"

"How about you, Hammond?" Frank asked.

119

pipeline security—

"These all so
Frank said. "Do
would want to stic

Hammond's fac
now. "I didn't w
mouth," he adn
money."

Now it was the
had kept your mo

"No, I just ke
said. "This whole
and I went along
idea where you co
up to?"

"Your guesses
his sneer taking in
doesn't matter. Y
allowed us to get i

"You dirty littl
bagman, but Fran

"Okay, that's e
the whole story s
authorities and—
The bagman was
ground.

"You'll never stop us!" he hissed. "And your authorities will never question me!"

Frank dropped to his good knee. But the bagman had already stopped moving—he lay rigid. Frank pried open the man's mouth, recoiling from a sharp stink. What looked like a dental filling fell out, a big piece—the whole crown of a tooth.

"Look at this!" Frank picked up the filling and held it up. Joe came forward cautiously, his weapon still trained on Hammond and his men.

His eyes opened wide in disbelief. "A hollow tooth!" he whispered.

"Obviously, it was holding a suicide pill," Frank said, his face grim.

"More spy stuff," Joe said, shaking his head.

But Frank Hardy's face grew grimmer. "Think for a second, Joe. What group has standing orders for its people to die rather than be captured?"

Joe looked even more unbelieving. "You're not thinking—the Assassins?"

They'd run into the Assassins before. In fact, this group of terrorists-for-hire had sent the Hardys on the most painful case of their career. An Assassin bomb had wiped out Iola Morton, Joe's girlfriend, in a ball of flame.

"Assassins—in Alaska?" Joe muttered. "Hard to take. But if you're right, we've got big trouble."

"Not just us," Frank said. "The whole country could be in for a bad time."

"What do you mean?"

A shiver ran down Frank's back. "Think about it. We all depend on the oil from the pipeline. And right now the whole maintenance staff—security and all—has been infiltrated by terrorists."

Chapter

16

Spike Hammond rose up on his knees, staring at the dead bagman. The businessman was obviously upset—he was terribly pale.

"Terrorists?" he mumbled. "Attacking the pipeline?"

Hammond looked as if someone had kicked the world out from under him. "You know, I always prided myself on being a working man, successful in business, going for the American dream. I started out as a roughneck in an oilfield, then worked my way up in the construction business. I thought I'd made it. . . ."

His voice tightened. "Then things went bad. The company lost money, we needed cash. And this deal came along." Hammond looked down again at the lifeless terrorist and then buried his

face in his hands. The
in stunned silence.

"I can't believe th
through his hands. "I r

"That's just it," Joe
Now what do you thin
of your mistake?"

Hammond pushed hi
head was still bowed ar

"And what about
he?" Joe asked. "We
and you lied to us."

"I didn't lie—I hone
pened to him." Hamr
managers. "Carter her
problem with some of t

One of the men in the

"I was told that so
money and were begin
got on the horn to No
they'd take care of it. T

"So you don't have a
Frank asked.

Hammond shook his
them—probably at thei
to have a big equipmer
but they had an explosi
all this started."

Frank leaned in when
sion, his face grim. "I

1

they kept Scott and let Doug go,'' he said. ''Scott was a demolitions expert in the army.''

''I don't understand,'' Hammond said.

''They got their hands on Scott right after an explosion wrecked their depot outside of town. I bet they lost more than equipment out there; I bet they lost their bomb expert in that explosion, too.''

''Bomb expert?'' Then the pieces clicked together for Joe. ''They're going to blow up the pipeline!''

Frank was now face-to-face with Hammond. ''How many people did you give jobs to? Where are they working?''

''It's hard to say,'' Hammond responded. ''We had a lot of requests. . . . And I don't know exactly where they all work.''

''So they could be anywhere along the line? Anywhere?'' Joe asked, as if it were impossible to imagine such a thing.

''I'm afraid so,'' Hammond admitted.

''So, as far as you know, your entire company is infiltrated by terrorists! Do you know what that means? It means that the Assassins can disrupt the entire world oil supply!'' Joe said.

''At the very least, they can upset the supply for our country,'' Frank said, frowning. ''How much of our oil comes from the Prudhoe Bay oil fields?''

''About fifteen percent,'' Hammond mumbled.

mond?'' Cindy sa
down the river.''
and stood near
Trans-Yukon.

Hammond cro
down, burying hi

''What can we
asked.

Another of his
you do that, it'll b

Joe looked at th
from under a roc
different reason.'

''Joe's right,'' F
realize this guy is
bly push their s
them to call off ar

''So what shou
again.

Frank looked a
and we'll need all
and your men con
ities will be easy
pipeline.''

''You've got o
men?'' Hammond

who were standing together, some distance from him. They stared at him blankly.

"Right, men?" he asked again.

The three looked at one another, then one of them stepped forward. He was called Carter, and he looked as if he had been elected to act as spokesman.

But as he passed Cindy, he dodged behind her. One of his arms whipped around her neck. A gun appeared in his other hand, and he pressed it to Cindy's head.

"Sorry, Hammond. No deal!" Carter said, holding Cindy in front of him like a shield. "Just give us the money and we'll get out of here."

Hammond stared at Carter. "Are you out of your mind?" he shouted. "Where are you going to go? You can't walk away from this!"

"Watch us," Carter said. "Right, guys?"

The other two managers grouped behind Cindy and Carter as Joe raised his gun.

"Don't try it, kid!" Carter shouted. "Just give us the money and no one will get hurt!"

Hammond looked at Frank and Joe.

"We've got no choice. Give them the bag," Frank said.

Hammond stepped forward, picked up the bag, and set it down in front of his managers. One of them reached out and picked it up.

"Don't do this!" Hammond begged. "We've got another chance. We can make up for our mistakes."

no matter what you try
want to rot with you.''

"That's not true,'' Fr

"Save it,'' Carter sna

He motioned with l
began to back up towar
per. Tanook, sensing s
gan to whimper. Carter

"You'd better keep tl
we'll kill him,'' he warn

Virgil put a hand on
dog fell silent.

"You can't do this
"Wake up and smell th
now, you'll go down ir
whole world will know
be after you for the rest

"What are you, runr
one of the managers sa
for us all to get away—
it on saving your crock

The three managers
ward the chopper. On
scrambled to the doors.
continuing to hold Cind

"Throw your guns ov

1

the barrel of his revolver harder into Cindy's temple.

Joe and Frank put the safety switches on and tossed their weapons forward. The side door of the chopper slid open, and Carter stepped up, still dragging Cindy along.

"You're not taking her!" Joe yelled. "There's no point!"

"I'll toss her out when I'm ready," Carter yelled back. "Just keep your distance and everything will be all right!"

Joe and Frank watched as the engine of the chopper coughed to life. The blades began to rotate. They could still see Cindy, standing by the side door of the helicopter, Carter holding a gun to her head.

At the last minute, as the chopper began to lift from the ground, Carter gave Cindy a shove. She landed on her feet and then fell onto her hands. She half ran, half crawled to avoid the overhead blades.

The copter lifted rapidly, rising to a height of thirty feet. Carter was still standing in the open hatchway, laughing down at the Hardys, Hammond, and Virgil.

And just at that instant a huge noise erupted within the chopper's belly. The helicopter exploded. Its thin walls blew out, and the rotary blades wobbled wildly into space. The sky filled with glass and chunks of metal. Huge pieces of

fiberglass spun th
Frisbees.

Where there ha
there was now a
around the flames

On the ground J

Pieces of wreck
the sky to pierce t

Chapter

17

JOE AND CINDY were protected under a dead bush as the sky gradually emptied itself of debris. Frank, Virgil, and Tanook had found shelter of a sort behind the boulder. Only Hammond remained standing, looking on in stunned silence. Perhaps he thought he was atoning for what he had done.

"I don't believe it," he said over and over, shaking his head. "What happened?"

"The money bag must have been booby-trapped," said Joe. "As soon as they reached a certain height, a detonator set off the bomb. It was meant for you, too," he said to Hammond.

The big redheaded construction boss swallowed hard. "You mean they were going to get rid of us?"

"That's right," Frank said. "You'd served

your purpose. They didn't want you around to talk and foul things up. Human life means nothing to them. Not even their own!"

"The scary thing is, Scott probably made that bomb," Joe remarked.

"But we still haven't found him—*and* we've got to stop the people who have him now," Frank announced. "Any ideas where we should start?"

Cindy spoke up. "I'm pretty certain most of the North Slope people were hired as hatch men. They open the hatches on the pipe and make sure everything is going smoothly."

Joe looked at her. "You didn't say that before."

"I just remembered that that was what I usually typed on their personnel records."

"Then that's it!" Frank said. "They've put bombs in the hatches. Anything else you remember?"

Cindy frowned, trying to force anything else out of her memory. "Most of them started working down south, near Valdez. Lately, they've been working in the north, toward Prudhoe."

Frank nodded. "They probably worked their way right up the pipeline. And now, if they've got to get out of here quickly, they're in range of that submarine up north."

He stood up. "We've got to get to the pipeline and take a look. Virgil, can you fix that chopper?" He pointed to the Assassin's helicopter, with the parachute snagged in its rotors.

"Right away," Virgil said. He leapt up on the top of the enemy bird and began to unravel and cut away the mess. "We could hike down the mountain and use mine," he called out as he worked. "But I think it'd take too much time."

"You're right," Frank said. "We've got to act fast."

Frank, Cindy, and Hammond gathered rocks to pile over the dead Assassin's body. When the temporary grave was completed, Cindy took a moment to mutter a few words in prayer.

Suddenly the chopper engine roared to life. Virgil waved from the pilot's seat. They ran over and climbed aboard, grateful for Virgil's expertise. They rose straight up from the mountaintop, then swooped to the south.

They gained speed and rose up again to get over the Brooks Range. In the early-morning light, the desolate area below seemed totally untouched by humans. But after a brief flight, they were flying over what seemed to be a miles-long brown snake, coiling over the rolling terrain.

It was a service road cut into the virgin landscape. And next to it was the gleaming pipe, stretching as far as the eye could see.

Hammond pointed out the first inspection hatch.

Virgil put the chopper down on the service road. Dust billowed around them as they jumped from the chopper and approached the pipe. Hammond reached out and touched the hatch.

"You need a special tool to unlock these babies," he said. "I didn't think about that."

"Wait a minute," Joe said. "I saw something in the back of the copter." He trotted over and reached behind the passenger seat of the Assassin's copter. Standing up, he held up an unusual-looking wrench.

"Is this what you're talking about?"

"Bingo," Hammond cried, and he began to unlock the hatch. After several minutes, he unscrewed the final bolt. But the hatch didn't budge. "Stuck," Hammond growled.

He attacked it again and, with a huge burst of strength, threw the hatch open. Then he stuck his head inside the hole.

"Don't see a thing," he said, his voice echoing inside the pipe. "Looks fine to me."

"Let me see," Frank said. He joined Hammond at the edge of the opening. Peering into the darkness, Frank could see nothing. The fierce smell of oil made his head swim, and all he heard was the velvety gurgle of the dark stream rushing inside the pipe.

Suddenly a loud click sounded in the dark. It seemed to come from the inner wall. Frank glanced to his right and saw something large and heavy splash into the river of oil. He grabbed for it, but he couldn't reach it.

"Something just fell off the wall of the pipe,"

"Grab it," Joe said.

Frank held up a filthy hand. "I tried, but it's gone."

"There shouldn't be anything hanging inside the pipe," Hammond said. "And there's nothing to hang it on."

"A magnet would hold on to the pipe," Joe said.

Frank nodded. "Probably an electromagnet that could be turned off by a radio transmitter. I'll bet they still use them in the military."

His face darkened. "Scott again! They've probably got one of those mines at every hatch."

"And they've just set them all free now," Joe said. "They're floating in the oil. When they get to the right spots, they'll probably go off."

"When they get to the pumping stations!" Hammond said. "We're not just talking about some holes and huge oil spills. They want to rip the guts out of the whole system!"

"Where must we go to stop this?" Virgil asked.

"I'll bet they've set themselves up inside a pumping station," Frank said. "That way they can monitor the flow of oil to make sure the mines have reached the most vulnerable locations."

Hammond spoke up. "I hate to say it. I sold them the construction plans to the main pumping station up in Prudhoe. One of their guys is the plant supervisor." He hung his head.

"That's it!" Frank said. "Let's go!"

The copter thundered through the air toward

the pumping station. Hammond was determined to do his part to make up for his mistake.

"I know the place inside and out," he said. "I worked on the crew that built it." He turned to Virgil. "Land on the roof. We can go down the climate-control vents."

Virgil nodded. He brought the chopper over the station and settled it down on the flat asphalt roof. Joe jumped out, and Frank cautiously followed. Hammond started to go, too.

"We'll take care of this," Joe said. "Stay with Virgil and Cindy. We need you on lookout."

"What about Frank's leg?" Virgil yelled down.

"It's about ninety percent, Virgil," Frank yelled back.

Hammond reluctantly agreed to let the boys go alone. "Okay. Just rip off those screens," he said, pointing to the large, chimneylike outlets on the roof. "You can slide down the ducts. The different rooms are labeled on the inside. You'll probably want the control room." He gave quick directions.

"Thanks," Frank called. "Now get out of here, fast!" Hammond jumped back in the copter, and Virgil took off.

The Hardys wasted no time. Joe ripped the screen off one duct and climbed in, followed by Frank, who could only crawl on one knee. The other leg he dragged behind him. It was dark inside, but when they came to a vent, light shone in from the space below. They could hear the

136

constant drone of the pumping machinery deep inside the building.

Sometimes, as they crawled along, muffled voices drifted up from the various rooms they passed. Frank and Joe were careful to make no noise as they crept through the darkness.

Following Hammond's directions, they dropped down several levels and crawled over the center of the building. Finally they reached a vent marked "Cntrl. Rm."

The floor was a long way down when they peered through the vent. They were in a high-ceilinged room containing a control booth filled with computer equipment. Two men stood in front of a large panel of controls.

Joe tapped Frank on the shoulder, then pointed. There was another vent in the room, directly over the booth. They crawled until they could lean over the small grid that covered the opening.

They listened to the voices below.

"So, my friend, it's just a matter of minutes before the project is completed." It was the voice of Sandy White. Frank pressed his face against the grid, trying to see who the other person was.

"It's Scott," he whispered to Joe. "It's Scott and Sandy White!"

They listened again.

"Once I push this button, we'll be on our way to the sub. The crew here is on coffee break, so they'll never know what happened. By the time

the cramped spa[ce]
through the hole.

He flew into V[ ]
the control panel[ ]
across the floor.[ ]
"Scott, we're frie[ ]
had time to say.

White was imm[ ]
ming an elbow [ ]
groaned and dou[ ]
breath. But every[ ]
fused to expand.[ ]
ner, unable to dec[ ]

Frank came do[wn]
but White was re[ ]
Frank landed. Bu[ ]
knocked the foot[ ]
grabbed it, twisti[ng]
White to the grou[nd]

White twisted h[ ]
self with the foot[ ]
Frank in the face [ ]

Frank's head snapped back, and he fell, losing his hold.

White fell to the floor but sprang up immediately and ran for the control panel—or rather, for the little radio transmitter with the big red button that lay there. Joe tackled him and brought him down. But he couldn't pin the man. White wriggled out of Joe's grip, leapt to his feet, and raised his foot to stomp Joe on the neck.

Joe rolled out of the line of fire, and White's foot only scraped the side of his head. His ear felt as if it had been ripped off. White again went for the detonator, but this time Scott stepped in. He snatched it away from White and threw the transistor pack to Frank.

White went after Frank but then stopped.

"Okay, enough," he said, taking a similar pack out of his pocket. "Your friend here is wired with enough plastic explosive to wreck this room. He's a human bomb! And this is the detonator!" He held the small transistor box in his right hand. "Now give me the switch to the mines, or I'll kill all of us right now."

Frank looked at Scott. He could see the unmistakable lump taped to his stomach.

"That's right," White said. "Just like the persuader I used on you. Now give me the switch before I use this one!"

Frank stared into the madness behind White's eyes.

139

"Give it to
his neck bulg

Frank had
were capable
a big cheese
make that sa

"If you fli
pipeline will
Frank poppe
hand and rip
Give up!"

When Whi
looked like a
But his mov
and backed
holding up th

"Stay whe
take your fri
more damage

Chapter

18

JOE LUNGED FOR the door, but his brother grabbed him.

"Let them go," Frank whispered roughly.

"Are you out of your mind?" Joe yelled. "He's about to escape. He may even kill Scott just for kicks."

Frank continued to hold his brother back. "He's less likely to do that if he thinks he's won. Let's give him a chance to escape."

They ran to the door and watched as White dragged Scott across the floor of the station.

"See?" Frank told Joe. "We've left his plan in ruins. The mines are useless now, without this." He held up the detonator, its wires and microchips hanging out like an electrician's nightmare.

"And we know another thing. White isn't about

to risk his own life. He proved that in here just now.'' Frank stared out as the terrorist dragged his captive into the maze of pumping machinery.

"Yeah, but we're going to lose sight of him, Frank! If he can stash Scott somewhere and get out of the building, he could still trigger the bomb, kill Scott, and do some serious damage.'' Joe pounded the wall in frustration. Then he stopped. A blueprint of the entire station was thumbtacked right where his fist had landed.

"Check this out!'' Joe said.

"Quick,'' Frank said, when he saw what it was. "Where are the exits?''

"Looks like there're only three, aside from the main one,'' Joe stated.

"Remember where they are. Now let's go. We've given him enough time.''

They broke through the door and practically fell down the flight of stairs that led from the control booth to the floor of the pumping station.

"He went this way!'' Joe called as he sprinted across the cement floor toward a jungle of pipes and machinery.

Frank followed behind as fast as he could, casting a worried look at the incredibly complicated mass of hardware, with its hundreds of hiding places.

"Maybe I took a chance letting him go. But I

didn't want to push him too far,'' Frank said as they pushed into the steel jungle.

Joe was in the lead, but he skidded to a stop when the floor ended. Looking over the edge, they could see two or three stories down. The entire space was filled with pipes, painted green, red, and orange.

Frank stared down in shock. "That's a bit more hiding space than I counted on."

The network of pipes filling the vast, dark space looked like the inside of a giant mechanical stomach. Miles and miles of bent, wandering tubes were all humming and gurgling with life.

But Joe wasn't interested in the looks of the place. His eyes were straining for any sign of motion. "There they are!" His arm stabbed down into the dimness.

"I see them." Following Joe's arm, Frank instantly caught sight of White and Scott. They looked like miniature figures climbing through a maze of giant tree trunks.

Joe leapt out onto the first pipe and began to swing to the next one like a monkey. Frank followed, using his arms the whole way.

"He's taking him down to one of the big compressors," Joe said, leaping from one pipe to the next.

Frank glanced down and saw them struggling through the endless labyrinth of twisting metal. Scott seemed to have a rope connecting him to White.

Joe sprang recklessly from pipe to pipe, landing on the narrow surface of one, then crouching down and lowering himself to the one below. It's a lucky thing we have sneakers, he thought.

When he landed on a pipe without a handhold available he had to keep his balance and not think about what a fall would mean. The image of being knocked from pipe to pipe until he reached the distant floor wouldn't help keep him steady.

Frank followed more slowly, going hand over hand, keeping his cool in a deadly situation.

"Do you see them?" he asked.

Dropping onto a pipe, Joe peered down. "He's reached the compressor, and he's tying Scott to a pipe." He glanced up at Frank. "I'm going after White. You go for Scott—get the bomb off him."

Joe took chances, dropping farther, straining to catch pipes. Once he bounced off a tube he'd aimed for and nearly went tumbling down through the maze. But he managed to grab on to another pipe and hang there for a moment, catching his breath. Looking down, he realized he'd nearly reached the compressor.

Below him, White was scrambling around on a large pipe, lashing Scott down. Scott fought against the ropes, but he was obviously scared about setting off the bomb on his stomach.

White tied the final knot around Scott's neck and looked up. Seeing Joe coming fast, he leapt off the big pipe like a spider monkey. Catching a

144

thin pipe several yards away, he swung himself down into the darkness like Tarzan and silently disappeared.

Joe covered the last of the distance to Scott's pipe with a series of hair-raising jumps. He landed on all fours about a yard away from where Scott was tied.

"Scott, my brother's coming to help you out. I'm going after that maniac," he yelled. "Frank's coming."

Scott nodded, but Joe could see the panic in his eyes. The poor guy must be half out of his mind by now, Joe thought. He's been a captive for almost a month, building bombs for terrorists—and now he's a human bomb.

Joe continued his wild descent. Sandy White was still ahead of him, dashing through the tangle of pipes at the bottom of the station. He'd reached the floor but still had to climb over some broad feeder pipes as he headed for a side door.

Joe realized that White had made a mistake by going straight down. He still had to struggle across the floor. And that gave Joe a chance to catch up. He began angling his way down through the overgrown monkey bars, cutting a course to just above the doorway.

He glanced back. Frank had reached Scott and was struggling to untie him, balancing on the pipe and tugging at the knots at the same time.

Now it was up to Joe to win the race to the

door. Joe remembered from the blueprint how this door led to a flight of stairs up to ground level and an exit to the pumping station. The area outside the station was open space.

Joe figured White would want to run a good way before finally detonating the bomb. He wouldn't know how far the exploding compressor would throw debris and would want to be a good distance from the building. Joe bore down, leaping and swinging through the pipes, almost in a trance now, knowing that his brother and Scott were depending on him.

White reached the door just seconds before Joe was in position to drop on him. The terrorist rammed into the exit with his shoulder, setting off an alarm.

Neither of them paid any attention to the shrill, bone-jarring siren. Joe swung down by the doorway and pushed through. He knew White was probably running up the stairs to the exit.

Clawing his way up the steps, Joe could feel his lungs burning with desperate fatigue. Now there was another door ahead of him. He rammed through to find a wide, empty space outside the building.

There was White, sprinting toward a helicopter with the North Slope logo. His escape vehicle had parked far out from the building. Its engine was already running, and a side door was open. White glanced over his shoulder, saw Joe, and forced his pace a bit faster. Joe didn't know if he could catch him. He only knew he had to.

From above came the clattering sound of another chopper. Joe looked up. It was Virgil. Spike Hammond stood in the open bay with the MAC-10 in his hands.

The North Slope pilot saw them, too. He turned up the throttle and lifted a few inches off the ground. Obviously he expected Sandy White to dive into the chopper headfirst, and then he'd take off.

Joe heard a shot. The engine of the North Slope chopper screamed to a halt. The blades whirred around helplessly, and the nose of the copter smashed into the ground. Hammond had hit a bull's-eye.

White stumbled to a halt. Joe could see his chest heaving as he tried to catch his breath. The men in the damaged chopper bailed out of the open door and made a run for it. White watched his comrades scatter. He looked up to see Virgil's copter hovering. He faced Joe, who was sprinting toward him.

A thought flicked across Joe's mind as he sprinted toward White: This is where an Assassin is the most dangerous, when he's got nothing to lose and nowhere to go.

For a second Joe couldn't figure out why White was just standing there. Then he watched as the terrorist's hand flashed into his pocket. It came out with the detonator.

A surge of joy erupted through Joe. He bore down on White like a freight train. Frank had done his job; now it was Joe's turn. He was going to take this Assassin alive!

White threw the detonator switch away and bit down on something in his mouth—hard.

He's got a hollow tooth—and a suicide pill! thought Joe as he forced a little more speed out of his aching legs.

But White didn't go into convulsions in front of Joe. Apparently he was having trouble with the cap on his tooth. He was yanking on it with his fingers as he backed away from Joe.

Joe barreled up, realizing he'd have just one shot at stopping this guy. Still running full tilt, he reared back, then unleashed his right fist in a wild haymaker with all his weight behind it.

He caught White in the side of the jaw, snapping his head to the side. One punch was all he needed. White was out. And the poison pill was on the ground. Joe's punch had jarred the hollow tooth loose. When the Assassin was flung back, the tooth cap—and its deadly little filling—flew out of White's mouth.

Frank and Joe sat on either side of Scott as they waited for their plane at the airport. Cindy was with them, too. "I can't believe what you guys have done," she said. "It was nice of you to let Mr. Hammond turn Sandy White in."

Frank shrugged. "Yeah, well—he was pretty upset once he realized how he had been used. And he was in pretty deep trouble. This might help him. He'll probably still go to jail, but he won't have such a guilty conscience."

Joe grinned. "By the way, who's in charge of Trans-Yukon?"

"All the men who were fired came back and elected someone to run the company. They offered Scott a big job," Cindy said, smiling.

Scott Sanders shook his head till his long dark hair tumbled into his brown eyes. He looked like a young, handsome kid—until you saw the dark bags and fatigue under his eyes.

"No way!" he said. "All I want to do is go home and see my folks. Give me some time. Maybe I'll come back in a couple of months."

"Did they really give you a hard time?" Cindy asked sympathetically.

"Well, they lost all their explosives experts when they had an accident, so they kept me working pretty hard. I was tired, which is not the way to be when you're fooling around with

149

Joe patted him on the back. "We're just glad it worked out, and that we were able to stop those crazies. The authorities are collecting all the mines. And it turns out White is a big cheese in the Assassins. Once they've gotten all the info out of him, they hope to put a big dent in our friendly neighborhood terrorists."

Their plane was announced, and they began to gather their belongings.

Joe took Cindy by the hand. "If you'd like to come to Bayport sometime, let me know." He grinned. "We're not all that far from New York."

Cindy smiled. "Well, I was thinking about going to college in the East—who knows?" She shrugged. "It sounds good, but awfully far away."

"Far away from Alaska, maybe," Joe said. "But you'd be a lot closer to the rest of the world." Everyone laughed.

"Where's Virgil?" Frank asked, looking around. "He said he'd be here. We didn't have a chance to say goodbye."

"I don't know," Cindy said. "But you'd better go. Please write!"

Frank and Joe and Scott trudged across the tarmac to their plane. At the foot of the stairs, the attendant took their bags and stowed them in the baggage compartment. They climbed aboard and took their seats.

As the plane began to taxi toward the runway Scott and the Hardys looked out the windows and saw Cindy waving from the observation deck.

Then the plane took off, and they were on the way home.

Frank leaned back in his seat, finally able to relax—until he glanced out the window. "What's that?" he asked, pointing to a speck in the sky.

"Looks like a helicopter." Joe's voice was casual, but he sat up straight. The chopper came closer and closer to the plane. Could it be a revenge attack from the Assassins?

It was close enough now to see inside the pilot's bubble.

"Holy smokes!" Joe laughed. "It's Virgil!"

The native Alaskan was grinning broadly as he waved goodbye to his friends.

"Look, there's Tanook," Frank said. "He's in the passenger seat!"

Tanook sat tall and proud next to his master. His pink tongue was hanging out of his mouth, and his fierce blue eyes stared quizzically at the passing plane. Frank and Joe laughed. Tanook's head cocked to the side, and then he seemed to bark.

"So long, Tanook!" Frank said.

"So long, Virgil," Joe said quietly, almost to himself.

The chopper pulled away. In a matter of seconds it was lost in a bank of clouds.

Frank and Joe's next case:

Sparks fly when "Biker" Bob Conway roars into Bayport, looking for Frank and Joe. The motorcycle racer needs their help to prove his innocence in a hijack case. The problem is, Biker just escaped from jail. To make things worse, some very dangerous people are looking for him. One is a bounty hunter; the others are members of a motorcycle gang called the Sinbads. The Hardys can't leave a friend in trouble, and they defy their father in taking Biker's case. The brother detectives burn rubber in a high-speed race with both sides of the law . . . in *Nowhere to Run,* Case #27 in The Hardy Boys Casefiles™.